No Spoons Left

By Phoebe Jacobs

The author of this book is not a qualified medical professional. While efforts have been made to ensure accuracy and comprehensiveness, some medical advice and descriptions of symptoms and conditions may diverge from reality. It is important to note that this book is not a replacement for seeking professional medical guidance:

Phoebe Jacobs
Cover by Phoebe Jacobs
ISBN: 9781616279066

Phoebe Jacobs

No spoons left

Disability isn't a choice,

acceptance is.

September

Ellie

It starts about an hour after I wake up. I love that one hour of total control over my body. Then the twitching starts. My head jerks, my eye rolls, and my arm twitches. I take place at the dining table. My parents are seated on one side, and my little sister and I sit on the other. My forks and knives have been replaced with plastic ones. Around my plate, there are scratches and punctured holes in the pale wooden table that my tics put there. I call it my ticcy art. I spend that glorious hour in the morning doing my makeup. Perfectly winged eyeliner. With my plastic fork in hand, I take a big scoop of my oatmeal, which I don't make myself because it's simply not safe. My head twitches to the right side and I let out a few "humphs." It's another day of living with Tourette's.

I was diagnosed at the age of twelve. I'm fourteen now. It started with just little twitches. I'd scrunch up my nose, blink repeatedly, and move my mouth in weird ways. Throwing my head back or shaking vigorously. I wished for it to stop but it only got worse. Because then the vocal tics started, mouth pops, humphs, and eventually words. Bitch! Cunt! Sluts in slippers! It's behind you! Only one in ten people dealing with Tourette's has coprolalia, and I happen to be one of them. But now I must focus on eating this oatmeal without making the biggest mess. I'll probably fail.

"First day of high school, aye?" my dad says with his mouth full of cereal. My dad is so goofy and childlike. His head is bald and shines like a bowling ball. I let out a 'humph' and scrunch up my nose. "Don't remind me," I chuckle nervously. "You'll be okay, baby," my mother comforts me, laying her hand on my arm. "Well, I'm a big girl! I'm going to elementary school!" my little sister says with triumph. Her hair is even more orange than mine. Her blue eyes twinkle with excitement. "Yes, you are!" Mom encourages my little sister Mai. "Both my girls are grown up!" Mai chuckles and chomps on her toast and Nutella. "Well," my dad says, and slaps his hands onto his thighs in a funky rhythm. "We have to leave soon."

I watch my dad's red Fiat drive away. Behind me, there's a whirlpool of students. The noise is making my ears ring and my chest tingles with anxiety. I let out another 'humph' and twitch my neck. *Please be kind to me.*

I sit down at the far corner of the small assembly hall. The seats are dark blue and go up. Shoes shuffle and squeak on the pale hardwood floor. In the middle of the hall, there's a stand with a microphone and a few teachers wait patiently for the stream of students coming in to stop. I let out another 'humph' but cover my mouth with my hand, trying to disguise it as a sneeze. The hall is so loud, and the overhead lights buzz, making my skin crawl with anxiety. I put my hand on the blue seat below me. Then I tap with each finger. One, two, three, four, five. No that didn't feel right. Again. One, two, three, four, five. No! Again! One, two, three, you tapped it too long! One, two, three, four, five. There we go. I take a deep breath, trying to calm the whirlwind inside me. My eyes stray down to my black backpack. It's right in there. I don't have to hide. It's *right* in there. I bite my lip and blink my eyes. Fuck this. I grab my backpack, looking for the Sunflower lanyard. I pull it out from beneath my notepad and take a second to inspect it. The green card with the sunflowers on it. "I have Tourette's" it reads. I take a deep breath and quickly put it on. I don't have to hide.

A tall lady with short blonde hair and a fancy suit steps up to the microphone. "Hello, freshmen," her voice sounds through the hall, echoing off the walls. "Can we all quiet down for a moment?" The chatter of students quiets down as the last echo sounds through the hall. Oh, God. There's the itching in my throat. My body is on fire as I try to suppress it. I whistle once, let out a loud 'humph' and before I know it "Fuck off!" My eyes widen as my heart rate spikes. There's laughter from the whole hall, including the girl sitting beside me. "Okay, settle down!" the woman says a bit annoyed. "Who thinks this is funny, huh?" the woman scans the crowd. "Go on," the girl beside me whispers. Her hair is streaked with purple. "Fess up." I look into her eyes; my heart is still pounding. I grab the Sunflower lanyard with shaky hands and hold it up for her. The girl quickly reads it, her eyes softening with what I feel is a hint of pity: "Oh!" she whispers. "Never mind, I apologize."

"Let's continue," the blonde woman says, taking the attention of the room back to her. "I hope everyone had a wonderful summer break! And I hope you're ready for your first year of high school." There's a sudden roar of clapping from the students. The sudden loudness makes me tic. "First of all, I want all of you to know that you all have a place here." I smile shortly at that comment. "You belong, you matter." She looks around the room for a moment. "Let's all learn great things, help each other, be there for each other, and create a beautiful community here within our school. I hope you all have a great first day!" She gives all of us a nod before leaving the stand. The students all clap and holler.

Jana

I pick at the tape on my face as I walk through the hallway. The tube tickles my nose and I take a second to move it around. Keeping my head down, I look at my feet coming in and out of vision. Right, left, right, left, right, left. With a single swing, I readjust the heavy backpack on my back. I make my way into the classroom, still looking down at my feet. Just like always, I take a seat at the back. And for the first time, I look up, across the classroom. I already know everyone in here, but no one knows me, not really. I'm just the girl with the feeding tube that never ever talks. Thanks to having a paralyzed stomach and selective mutism. My eyes lock with one of the lacrosse players. Liam. He smirks at me with a gleam in his eyes as he leans forward, and then starts mooing at me. Yes, like a cow. His friends laugh and join in. I look down at the pale desk and hold my hand at my cheek, trying to hide the birthmark that takes up pretty much half my face. Our teacher, Mr. Rods, walks in. "Okay, Liam! We're not on a farm here!" The mooing finally stops.

Ellie

The walk to class is long, or at least, I made it long. The hallways are almost completely quiet except for the few students still lingering by their lockers. I look at the papers in my hand, twitching my head to the side, and let out a 'humph.' My first class is at the end of this hallway. As I get near the classroom my heart rate spikes and my palms sweat all over. They're going to laugh. They're going to judge. They won't understand. I'll be a freakshow. At last, my dragging feet come to a stop. I look at the pale wooden door in front of me and whistle once. Let's do this. Just suppress and you'll be fine. I knock on the wood twice. "Come in," a faint voice sounds from behind the door. I take a deep breath and push myself to open the door. The teacher looks up at me and I look back at him. “Ellie Montel?” he asks. I nod. The tension in my body is building up, needing to tic so badly. The electricity surges through my spine. And then it happens. I clap my hands twice. Twitch my head while I go “Hey!” in a high-pitched voice. I flip off my teacher and go “Faggot!” and then they calm down again. I *hate* ticcing slurs. There’s loud laughter in the classroom. But I’m too busy trying to not let the tears out and calm the tremor in my body. “Settle down!” the teacher yells loudly. The classroom dies out slowly. “Sorry,” I say softly. “I have Tourette’s.” The tall man gives me a pitiful smile. I hate that type of smile. “I know, don’t worry about it.” I ‘humph’ and twitch before walking to the back of the class and sitting down, ignoring the stares and whispers. The male teacher starts introducing himself. I whistle twice and my neck twitches. My nails dig into my school desk as I try to focus on what the teacher is saying, but the aching in my body is the only thing on my mind. I flap my hands and click my tongue. I put my hand over my mouth. “Fuck off,” I muffle my tic. My hands flap uncontrollably, and I feel like a puppet on strings, being bossed around, having no say over what I do. “Cunt!” I yell loudly. My heart jumps through the roof, embarrassment flooding my freckled cheeks. There’s mostly laughter but then one girl in the crowd speaks up. “Can you shut up, spaz?” My heart sinks. *Spaz*. “Alex!” the teacher shouts. “What? I’m serious, how am I supposed to focus if she’s just going to do that all of the time?" Tears sting my eyes once again, but I won't let them out, even with the lump growing in my throat, they won't see me cry. I knew this wouldn't end well. I wish to sit back at the table this morning, eating my breakfast and telling my parents I want to be homeschooled. My nails dig even deeper. "Gilles de la Tourette," the teacher says slowly, I look up at him unclenching my jaw, as he turns around, his back to us. He grabs the pencil for the smartboard and writes in bold letters: TOURETTES. "What is Tourette's?" he asks and scans the classroom from above his glasses. "It's this thing where people basically swear all the time," a girl's soft voice sounds. "Is it?" the teacher looks me straight in the eyes. I let out a 'humph' once again and then shake my head. "No."

"But you do swear right?" he says as he sits down on the corner of his desk. I take a deep slow breath. "When people with Tourette's swear, *fuck*, swear, it's called coprolalia. But only ten percent of people with Tourette's have coprolalia, me being a part of that ten percent."

"I thought it was a TikTok trend, like seriously, everyone's faking, how do we know you're not?" a tall dark-blonde girl says as she looks me dead in the eye. "I've had tics for many years and have an official diagnosis. I'm not faking, I would never fake this. Cause honestly, it's a living hell," I softly smile at the girl but there isn't much understanding in her dark eyes. "But you can control it right?" the teacher goes. I shake my head. “No, it’s completely involuntary. If I could stop, I would. I don’t like making these noises any more than you like hearing them.”

“What can we do to help you?”

“C-cunt!” my tics go. “Just, treat me like everyone else. I’m a person too. Tourette’s isn’t a choice, but acceptance is.”

The teacher smiles at me and winks quickly. “We’ll accept you, won’t we?”

“Hell, yeah we will!’ a slender girl with pitch-black hair smiles at me.

Jana

I sit down on the soft pastel blue chair; playing with the little cotton balls that linger on it. Grabbing them between my thumb and index finger, rolling them, and then flicking them to the floor. My tablet is resting on my thighs. Mrs. Laurence takes a seat on the less comfortable-looking chair. She puts a notepad on her thighs, that’s where she’ll write down what I’ll say to her through my tablet. “So, Jana, how is your first day going.” I shrug and flick another cotton ball. “Do you have any idea when you’ll get your gastrostomy tube?” I shake my head but never look her in the eyes. “I remember last school year you said you weren’t quite a fan of the nasojejunal tube. You were scared people would make fun of it?”

I let that sink in for a moment but decide no response is the best way to go. I flick another cotton ball. "Can you use your tablet to communicate with me please?"

I shrug. "There must be something you want to tell me." I take a deep breath and unlock the tablet. I type quickly with my fingers and let the device speak for me. "They still call me a cow because of my birthmark,' the monotone voice of the lady inside my tablet says. "Is it still Liam and his friend?" I press the button and the tablet goes "Yes."

"Do you want me to talk to him?"

"No," the tablet goes.

"How do you feel about your birthmark?"

I type three letters and my tablet goes: "Moo."

I sit down at the lunch table by the trash cans. No one wants to sit here except for me. It's just the furthest away from everyone else. It's not like I eat lunch anyway. The ugly tube stuck to my face does that job for me. I have Gastroparesis, which basically means my stomach is partially paralyzed. That's why I need this nasojejunal tube, so I don't starve to death. Soon, I'll be getting my gastrostomy tube. Which is a feeding tube placed directly into my stomach. They'll make a small incision and shove it in there. Don't you just love life?

Ellie

I walk through the cafeteria, nervously looking around. The noise of it all overtakes me. My twitches get worse and worse. My neck jerks, scrunching up my nose, clap, clap, clap, humph, humph, whistle. “Yo!” a loud voice sounds from across the room, standing out above the rest. Twitch, clap, whistle. “Yo, spaz!” *Oh no, he means me.* I look at where the voice came from. It’s a big dude with broad shoulders and dark hair. I twitch again and he mimics it, making fun of me. “Weirdo!” he yells out. I twitch and humph. “Yo can you stop?! Fucking spaz.” Tears tickle my eyes for the third time today; I whistle once again. I can’t do this. I one-eighty and walk towards the exit.

I stand at the edge of the parking lot. Twitching and ticcing. Impatiently waiting for the redness of our Fiat to drive through all the other cars. I wiggle my leg. I tap my fingers to my thumb. Index, middle, ring, pinky, index, middle, ring, pinky. I repeat this five times and then let a deep breath out. There it is, the glorious red of our Fiat. As I get into the shotgun seat my dad smiles at me. “How did it go?” I shrug. I twitch my neck, three times and go “F-fuck! Fuck, fuck, cunt fucker!” My little sister gasps from the backseat. “Bad words!” the ginger girl goes. My dad turns around to her, “You know your sister can’t help it.”

“I know!” her high-pitched voice sounds.

“Old bald man,” my tics go.

“Just bald man please,” my dad jokes and lightens the darkness that had been lingering around me all day.

“You’ll be okay honey.”

"People just don't get it," I shrug.

"There's going to be people that won't be nice about it, but a lot of people will. Believe me."

I smile at the man who raised me. "I know." I want to believe it but it's hard when everyday people make fun of you.

I throw my black backpack onto the ugly tile floor in our hallway before making my way into the dining room where I know my mom will be sitting. Mai rushes in front of me and grabs her Nintendo Switch Lite. I 'humph' once as I arrive at the dining table, along with a small head jerk. "How was school?" my mom asks me. I can feel the tension surging down my hands, letting it out with jazz hands. "It was- *fuck*! It was fine." The tics continue with rapid head nodding and an endless amount of 'humphs.' I get a breather. "Sorry," I breathe in and intertwine my hands. I press my lips together in an awkward smile. Mom's eyes soften. "You have to stop doing that."

"What? Tic?"

"No, saying sorry for your tics."

"Well, you're a cunt!" My tics respond. I shake my head. "Should I apologize now?" Momma gives me a quick smile, pulling me closer to her as she hugs me around my torso. "Why don't you get yourself something to eat?" My dad says as he lays his hands on my shoulders. I smile and nod. The tension and anxiety that's been lingering around me all day slowly disappear. I smile at the two people who will love me no matter what. The people who accept me fully.

I'm watching *the office* on our big TV. Mai comes running in as I take another bite of my birthday cake pop tart. The pink plate in her hand tilts slowly as she stops in front of me. The cat ears on her onesie flop back and forth. "Look I got biscuits!"

"I'll spit on your biscuits!" my tics exclaims. Mai frowns. "No!"

"Sorry," I smile at her. "I didn't mean that."

"I know!" she smiles brightly and plops down on the other couch. Then there's the tension again. I kick my leg. "Fuck, fuck!" head jerk. "Bitch! Bitch! Bitch! Woah!" An entirely separate entity that takes over my body with no warning or reason. I kick my leg again and aggressively slam my hands into the couch. My head jolts back, pain shooting throughout my entire neck. "F-f-f-fuck, fuck," Then the collarbone punching starts. My sister is suddenly beside me. "Ellie, are you all right? Do you need momma?"

I nod. "Yes." Mai puts her pink plate down and runs into the dining room disappearing out of sight. Meanwhile, I'm left twitching and ticcing. I'm a ticcing time bomb. My mom walks in, and I plead with my eyes. *Make it stop. Please make it stop*. She squats down beside me taking my hand. "You're okay, hun." But then I punch myself in the face and my mom quickly flies into action. She grabs both my arms, gently holding them down, trying to restrain me from doing harm to myself. I shake and shake and shake my head. “Don’t tic! Don’t tic! Don’t tic!” my tics demand themselves. “Woah!” I throw my head back once again. I rock my body back and forth, but the tension won’t stop. I just can’t stop ticcing. “Baby, baby, shh,” my mom tries to shush me, comfort me, and do whatever she can. But the only thing we can do is wait it out. “Sluts in slippers!”

“Okay, honey, okay, you’ll be fine. Just sit tight.”

It lasted over an hour.

My mom pulls the blanket over my tired body. I take a deep shaky breath. The attack has left me feeling drained and exhausted. My head keeps thumping, leaving behind a trail of pain with every single thump. Tears tickle the corners of my eyes. My mom pets my hair. I take another shaky breath and curl up my aching body. “I’m sorry mom, I know you didn’t want this.” To be honest, I feel like a burden. “My dear baby girl,” she smiles. “I love you, Tourette’s or not, I love you and you will always be my little girl.” She strokes my cheek and slowly stands up from her kneeling position. “Get some rest.”

Jana

My face is squished into my pillow, my tube has probably left a mark on my cheek. I let myself lie in a near slumber for a few more minutes. The morning sun gradually brightens up my room. It's time for another day. Groaning and huffing, I pull myself upright. I scratch through my hair and throw the thin blanket off from over my body. I lift my feet out of the bed onto the cool wooden board that is my floor. I clip my tube off the stand and drag it with me. The metal of the pole feels cool on my palm as it trails loudly behind me. I stroll down the hall into the small bathroom still half asleep. I unhook from the feeding bag tubing, get the old tube off, and take my syringe to flush my NJ tube. I open up my pump and get the cartridge from the last 24 hours out since I always replace my bags in the morning. I turn around and throw the old bag and tube in the special trashcan, specifically put there for my bags and tubes. I open the mirror cabinet and take out my anti-depressants and anti-anxiety medicine, and I can't forget the meds for my Gastroparesis. I swallow them one by one. I grab my new bag and a carton of what is my food and pour it in there, letting it go through the tube before hooking it to my pump. I watch the beige liquid flow through the tube, into my nose, to my digestive system. All set for the day.

Ellie

My eyes scan the cafeteria. The tables are filled with loud teenagers that make me want to eat in the toilets again. I take a deep breath, twitch, turn around and start walking. "Ellie!" a voice sounds through the crowd.

It's probably a different Ellie. "Ellie!" it sounds again. I come to a sharp stop and dare to turn around. Once again scanning the cafeteria. "Ellie! Over here!" I lock eyes with a tall, black-haired girl. She waves me over. I take a deep breath, pushing down the anxiety settling in my chest, and take steady steps toward her and the other girl sitting beside her. "Sit with us," she says kindly. Well, that is unexpected. I smile quickly, twitch, and sit down. "I know you from class," she says. "Me too," the other brown-haired girl says. "I'm Stephanie, but you can call me Steph." The black-haired girl goes. She has the brightest blue eyes; making her almost look surreal. "This is Miriam," she points at the other girl. "So, Tourette's hey?" Steph says. As if that's the only thing interesting about me. I smile and nod anyway, I'm sure she means well. Then I humph and whistle. "That's fine, we don't mind."

"Your hair is so pretty!" Miriam goes and grabs a strand of my wavy ginger hair. "Thanks," I smile a genuine smile at that comment. Whistle, twitch, scrunch up nose. "I have to be honest with you," Steph goes. "This school fucking sucks, okay? Mean seniors and sophomores and the freshmen are always the victims."

"Yeah, and I'm a freshman and a spaz," I chuckle.
"Don't worry," Steph winks. "We got your back."

"Yes!" Miriam squeals. "Besties!"
I smile at the two girls.

Jana

"We have to try and find a solution, make a plan, to prevent what happened last year, you understand that right?"

I shrug at Mrs. Laurence. She takes a deep breath. "You were absent for over four months in total during last year." I shrug again.

Mrs. Laurence leans forward folding her hands together. "Have you heard about the spoon theory?"

My eyebrows grow closer in confusion. I shake my head.

"It's a theory made about chronic illness and mental illness. So healthy people have the luxury of not having to allocate their energy throughout the day and picking and choosing when to use it. Whereas people, like you," she points at me as I carefully listen. "People with chronic and mental illnesses don't get that luxury. So, let's say a spoon is one unit of energy. You may think, one spoon is to get ready for work, another spoon to eat breakfast, a spoon to drive to work, a spoon to work, do you get it?"

I nod shortly, she picks up where she left off. "But people with chronic illnesses and mental illnesses have to use a lot more energy on what others might consider basic tasks. So, getting ready for work or school in your case is not one spoon. It's one spoon to get out of bed, another spoon to change your tube, a spoon to take your medication, a spoon to get dressed, make sure you have everything, drive to school, and be at school can take up a lot of spoons, now a healthy person at this point has only used four spoons while you'll already have used seven or more spoons. Do you get it?" I nod again. "A person with illness will run out of spoons a lot quicker than a healthy person. They have enough spoons for most days, while you've already run out before the end of the day. Now you could borrow spoons from tomorrow, right? But then tomorrow is left with fewer spoons. We want to help you have more spoons throughout the day."

I nod. *How will you do that?*

"If you need the extra rest, let us know, we made you this pass." Mrs. Laurence grabs a bright yellow card from her desk. It reads "No Spoons Left" in bold letters. "You wave this, you won't have to speak, just show the card and you'll be allowed to go to the nurse's office to rest."

I nod. I quite like this idea. A sentence pops up in my head, just a simple short sentence, begging to be let out. Pushing against my lips. I open my mouth; I want to speak so badly. But nothing comes out. Mrs. Laurence notices and shifts suddenly. She's waiting for me to speak. She wants me to speak. I try again, but my voice is not there. Instead, I take my tablet and write it down. I click the button. "I'm a spoonie now," the tablet says. Mrs. Laurence chuckles, but I know she's disappointed I didn't say it out loud.

Ellie

I walk over to the schoolyard; my tics are accompanying me like usual. I jerk my neck and blink my eyes. This will never stop. It seems like a lifetime ago, like a whole other lifetime. Everything changed all of a sudden and I don't understand. Not about one percent of the population yet I have it. It doesn't seem fair. But yet here I am. I have Tourette's, which confuses a lot of people. People don't understand. People will just judge instantly. But I swear, I didn't choose this, and I'd never want anyone else to deal with this. But here I am. I have Tourette's Syndrome.

I walk into the school building and get greeted by one of my teachers. "Had a nice weekend, Ellie?" she asks politely with a bright smile. I want to just nod and tell her yes but instead: "Fuck you, cunt!" I stop for a second and take a deep breath. "Yes, my weekend was okay." She smiles at me, maybe with a hint of pity in there. I smile back and start walking again.

"There she is! My favorite ticcy friend!" Stephanie exclaims loudly, which makes me tic. "I'm your only ticcy friend Steph." She frowns at me. "Ellie!" Miriam shouts as she smashes her homework into her bright blue locker. I roll my eyes; I already know what she wants. It's only been two weeks of high school, but these two girls mean the world to me. "Definition of a contrarian?" I sigh. "Me. Definition of lazy? You. Do your own homework will you." She sighs and waves her hair away from her face. Her eyes stray to somewhere behind me. I follow her gaze. "Incoming," Miriam whispers to me. "Don't let it get to you," Steph says under her breath. I look at Liam walking through the hallway. The guy thinks he owns the school but he's nothing more than a stupid bully. "Crazy girl!" He yells my way. He starts to fake twitches and in response, my real ones start. My neck jerks to the side repeatedly. I aggressively close my eyes and then start blinking. I try to figure out where my tension is forming, trying to be one step ahead of my tics, but that never works. He starts laughing. "Cunt looking fucking faggot!" my tics yell through the entire hallway. People are turning their heads towards us, people whispering and laughing. Liam looks angry at me and whispers to me as he passes by "Fucking crazy bitch." I look back at my friends. "It's okay Ellie, he's just an asshole."

I sit in biology next to Stephanie. She leans closer to me and whispers "What did the cell say when his sister stepped on his toe?" she chuckles. I look up at the front of the class making sure our teacher is too busy to catch us. I think for a second and then I let out a soft chuckle. "Auch mitosis?" Steph starts laughing softly. I spit out air. "What in the hell?" I laugh softly. "You ladies having fun?" The teacher shuts us up and we both freeze. "Care to share?" she says annoyed. And here it comes. My face jerks to the right again. "Fuck you!" My tics exclaim. She sighs loudly. "I have Tourette's, what's your excuse?" my tics force me to say. There's soft laughter from within the classroom. "Okay, settle down," the teacher demands us, and so we do.

I lay against my backpack on the grass field of our schoolyard. I let the warmth of the early September sun embrace me. "Fuck the patriarchy and fuck all man!" Steph replies to Miriam's question I didn't even pay attention to. "Jeez," I chuckle. "That's a bit harsh."

"No, no, no!" she yells out. "Listen to me! Men are disgusting, each and every one of them." She looks at both of us, one at a time. "Listen to me and you won't have to make the same mistakes I did. Men are liars, don't ever trust them, and don't ever send them nudes!"

"Cheers, where were you when I was growing up," Steph rolls her eyes. "Liam!" Ms. Conard yells throughout the entire schoolyard. "What is he doing?" Miriam says annoyed. I sit up on my elbows and watch the commotion. Liam is repeatedly kicking a ball into one of the windows. "He smacked me in the head with that ball last week!" Miriam's pissed-off child-like voice sounds. "He didn't even say sorry." I chuckle at my friend's comment. "Liam stop kicking that ball!" Ms. Conard continues. "You know ballgames are prohibited!"

"But I love balls!" my Tourette's says.

Liam keeps kicking the ball as it thuds, thud, thuds against the window. "I said stop kicking the ball!" He brings the ball to a stop underneath his right foot. "Not a problem." He picks up the ball and starts throwing it into the window instead. Throw, catch, throw, catch, throw, catch. "That's it, give me the ball!" the chubby woman spits. Liam catches it one last time and then walks over to Ms. Conard. "Here you go miss," he smiles politely before walking away. "What an actual cunt," I say loudly, and that was not a tic.

I whistle once throughout the quiet classroom. Steph is looking at her phone, hidden below the table. My head jerks back. "Bitch," my tics say. It's way too quiet in here which just makes it worse. Steph looks up at me. "Are you okay?"

"It's so quiet," I whisper back followed by a few humphs. "Oh my God, can you be quiet?" a girl from the far corner yells at me. The sudden noise makes me tic a few times. "If she could, she would," Steph defends me. "People are trying to actually learn stuff in here." I bite my lip at that comment. "Yeah, and I'm trying too, but my disability is not my choice." The girl frowns at me. "What disability? Just shut up."

"Okay, you two let's settle down," the ginger teacher demands us. "Bitch! Bitch! Bitch!" I yell out followed by another whistle. I grab my bag and jacket and hurry my way out of the classroom. I hate this. "Ellie?" Steph's soft voice sounds right before the door closes behind me.

The school bell rings, but I've been sitting in this bathroom stall for the last half an hour. The noise of a group of girls floods the washroom. I look down at my phone. I scroll through TikTok, looking at people spreading awareness for Tourette's. It's funny, isn't it? That it's called TikTok. I wish I could spread awareness. I wish I wasn't so ashamed of it. I just want people to accept me. I want people to know that Tourette Syndrome is not a choice, but acceptance is.

I sit at my desk, an empty piece of paper on it, a pen in my hand. I need to do something. Anything.

Ten things not to say to people with TS.

"Why don't you swear?" Only one in ten people with TS have Coprolalia. I do though.

"Do you really have TS?" Uh, yes. Next question.

DON'T MIMIC OUR TICS PLS

"You need to relax." I can literally not control it wtf?

"Can you be quiet?" You think I do this on purpose or something?

"You're being embarrassing." Jeez, thank you. Now fuck off.

"Are you mentally challenged?" TS is actually a neurological disorder, not a mental one.

"Isn't there medication?" There is but it's not a magical cure.

"Why don't you just stop?" Uh, because I literally cannot control it.

"You're weird." I'm different, not less.

My alarm clock wakes me from my deep slumber. My brain is alert and ready for the day. I jump out of bed and into my pink fluffy slippers. I run a hand through my hair as I walk over to my desk which is illuminated by the early sun. The sound of traffic already fills the air. I look at the single sheet of paper on my desk and bite my lip. *Am I going to do this? Am I really?* I shake my head and clear my thoughts. *I am.*

I sneak into my mom's office and sit down on the squeaky chair. I place the sheet of paper on the copy machine and watch the line of light scan it from underneath the plastic top. Then it starts buzzing and I watch the papers come out.

My parents are already eating breakfast as I walk into the dining room and take my textbooks that have been lying on the table since last evening's homework session. I struggle them into my heavy backpack.

"Good morning," my mom greets me once I make my way into the kitchen. "Morning," I smile and twitch once. “We should get going,” my dad says as he takes one more sip of his coffee. I walk over to my mom and kiss her on the cheek. “Have a nice day at school!” She yells after me. “I will!”

I make my way through the big school entrance which is even busier than I expected. I jerk my head back and blink my left eye. Then I spot them, my main girls. I take a small sprint over to them. “My favorite ticcy friend!” Steph says. I roll my eyes. “Your only one too.”

I dig through my backpack and slip out the fifty copies of the list I made and hold them up. Miriam looks up from her phone while Steph starts reading. “What’s that?” Miriam says monotonal. “We need to spread these all over the school.”

“Ten things not to say to people with TS. ‘Why don’t you swear?’ Only one in ten people with TS have Coprolalia. I do though. ‘Do you really have TS?’” Steph mumbles to herself. “What are you doing girl?”

“Spreading awareness.” I smile confidently.

“That’s badass!” Steph exclaims and holds her hand out. I give her a few of them. “Now we scatter them.”

I plop my last few sheets down in one of the girls’ washrooms right before the bell rings.

Principal Stanley slides the paper over to me. I look at my list and twitch a few times. She sits down on her chair. “Care to explain?” I shrug. And ‘whoa’ twice. “I just want to spread – bitch – awareness.”

She leans back and sighs deeply. "I know you're struggling with this," she taps the paper a few times. "But multiple teachers have complained about it causing a commotion in class."

"Okay, but it's important."

"It's important to you, but we don't need to bring all this to school."

I scoff. "But I live with this every day, and everyone treats me like shit because of it."

"Ellie, Ellie, Ellie, listen. Just no more of this," she circles her hands. "Okay?"

I bite the inside of my cheek, "Fine."

I stomp down the busy hallway looking at the ugly floor beneath my feet. My eyes go up and my heart drops. A girl appears in front of me. Tall, with a birthmark that covers about half of her face. A tube is taped to her cheek. She's hugging a tablet in a purple case closely. She walks past me, but I can't keep my eyes off her. I turn with her and watch her stroll away from me. Liam jumps in front of her. "Here's our cow!" He moos a few times before the girl walks away from him. Liam's eyes lock with mine. "What do you want? Spaz!" He spits at me.

Jana

I sit down at the back of the class. The room is filled with the chatter of the other students. The noise makes me want to crawl into a dark corner and cry. Liam comes walking in with his friends and he scans the room. Oh, God. He spots me and smiles sinisterly. He takes a sprint over to me and I almost go into fight or flight. He grabs something out of his backpack. They're cow ears. He puts the costume cow ears on my head and starts mooing. Everyone laughs. I bite my lip and take them off and throw them at the asshole. The teacher walks in and tells us to quiet down. I take my yellow spoonie card and hold it up. Mrs. Finley eyes the card and points her thumb toward the door. I get up and leave.

I lay down on one of the beds at the nurse's office. I turn and twist, but I will not cry. I will *not* cry. Mrs. Laurence pops up in the doorway. I sigh at her. "Are you okay?" I nod. "You're using your Spoon Card an awful lot." I shrug. "It's the last period. I called your mom; she's picking you up." I want to squeal and throw a party at that moment. But instead, I smile and give Mrs. Laurence a thumbs up. "Can you say one word?" she says carefully. "Just one?" I stare at her and swallow the lump in my throat. I open my mouth, and my lips part, but I just can't get them out. The words just won't come out.

"What do we have to do for you to speak at school?" my mom says softly as we both get into the car. I shrug. "They just won't come out."

"But you speak to me, you speak to your psychologist, why won't the words come out at school?"

"It's called selective mutism for a reason Mom," I say slightly annoyed. She stares at me as I stare back at her. "Well, can we go now?" I say loudly. She sighs before starting the car.

Ellie

I walk with my mom and Mai through the grocery store. There have been many stares so far despite me wearing my "I'm not possessed, I just have Tourette's" beanie. "Okay, so first time getting in trouble, that's new," my mom chuckles. "It was unfair, I should not have gotten in trouble for that."

"I know honey, I know."

I twitch as we walk past an older lady. She gives me a nasty stare. "Whatcha looking at, bitch?!" my tics exclaim. I sigh. "Mom this isn't fun, all I wanted to do is spread awareness."

"Well, maybe you should do it in a different way." She grabs some Fruit Loops. "No!" I shout. "I shall not be silenced!"

"Can I get some chocolate!" Mai says excitedly. My mom nods and smiles at her. "How was the rest of your day hun?"

I shrug. "I don't know."

"What did you learn today? What made you smile? What did-,"

"Jesus, Mom, please just stop."

She squints her eyes at me. "I don't see you angry often."

"Well, you're a bitch!" my tics yell out.

"Why thank you Tourette's."

I chuckle. "At least you understand."

I can't get her out of my mind. That girl. With the birthmark and feeding tube. She's like me. *Different*.

October

Jana

I lean my head against the window. The car shudders underneath me. We're on a road trip once again. Three days away from school, three days in a hospital. The car shudders again and my head lightly bonks into the window. I'm fidgeting with the tape of my tube again. This morning, I changed it to one with sunflowers on it. I look at the other cars whoosh by, the early sunrise lingers on the horizon painting colors of orange and pink. I close my eyes, hoping to drift into sleep again. So, when I wake up, I'll be at the hospital.

I softly get shaken out of my sleep by my mom's voice. "Honey, we're at the hospital."

I open my heavy eyelids; the orange tints of the sky have been replaced by blue. It's still very early in the morning. "Hmm," I go before stretching my body on the uncomfortable car seat. Let's go.

Hospitals are places where the sick are aided in their quest for restoration. How do they smell? Rather stuffy, warm, and antiseptic. It isn't very pleasant. In summer, the air conditioning helps to cool off the stuffy air. Winter is another story. Heated rooms are comfortable, but the hospital smell is just that: hospital, alcohol, gauze, and sickness. They could invest in freshening the area with something lavender or citrus, in my opinion. Yet, the hospital is kind of a home to us now. It doesn't smell good, but it sure smells like home.

We sit in the waiting room, waiting for my first procedure of the next three days. A gastric emptying scan. They do this for me every once in a while, to see how long it takes for my food to go into my intestines. I'm now in the waiting room. I just had to eat an egg and toast. Yes, I had to eat eggs and toast for this scan. Radioactive ones. There's an older couple in the corner, looking bored, maybe even more bored than I am. For the rest, the waiting room is empty. A young woman is sitting at the registration desk. Looking through papers and typing away on the PC. "Walker Jana?" a tall familiar man says from behind a door. My mom lets out a soft "Yes," before getting up, and I follow her. "Hello, Jana, how have you been?" Dr. Holland's eyes are shiny but there are wrinkles around them. His beard is stubbly, and his hair is wavy and messy. "I'm okay," I say softly. "Glad to hear that, well let's get started, shall we?" I nod.

I lie down on the uncomfortable plastic board. The machine is big and scary. I've done this many times, but it still freaks me out. There's a big X-ray above and below my stomach. Now we lay here for four hours.

Doing nothing, not moving. Fun, right? I close my eyes and listen to the machine whirring.

Ellie

I sit down at the table and grab a piece of toast. "Good morning," my mom says while sipping her coffee. "Morning." I take some butter and spread it on the toast with a white plastic knife. I whistle before taking a bite.

"Welcome to homeroom," Steph whispers quietly as she's filming the commotion that is our class's homeroom. She points her phone at me, I throw her a peace sign and then twitch my neck. "Okay but Hannah yesterday though," Miriam chuckles. "Oh no!" I say loudly. "Not when she called me Peppa because I had a snorting tic!" Miriam starts laughing and nods her head. "Like bro, it's either they hate on me for my Tourette's, or they think I'm the funniest person ever." Steph chuckles from behind her screen. "Can you stop filming me?" I say annoyed to her. "I'm trying to study!"

"You're the only person in here trying to study, the teacher is sick so we're in homeroom, enjoy the freedom!"

I squint my eyes at the black-haired girl. Then my tics slam my hand into my essay, scrunch it up, and throw it at Steph. "Fucking cow!" I yell loudly. Steph starts laughing and Miriam joins in. I pout my lips at my destroyed essay. Then I humph whistle and slam my fist into the table. I lean forward as my tics go: "Fuck you, you little shit."

"Oh, my God!" Steph loses it laughing. "I totally filmed that!" My tics twitch and shout and jerk. The commotion of the homeroom is making it worse. "Sluts in slippers!" I yell loudly. My friends basically die laughing. "Liam's got a boner!" Well, now *that*, made the entire homeroom lose it.

Jana

Time for day two.

We walk through the big entrance once again. I said it before, this really is my second home.

The nurse guides me through the halls as I try to keep up with her, but she has a fast pace. She opens the door to a small, very claustrophobic room. "Just get undressed and put on the hospital gown and then you can go out through the other door." She points to the door on the other side of the small room. I nod. I get dressed in the hospital gown and grippy socks. The two hospital tags on my wrist annoy me.

Time for an endoscopy, my least favorite procedure. I lay down on the procedure table, on my side. Just like always, they put a plastic guard in my mouth to keep it open. I absolutely hate this procedure even though it takes no longer than five minutes. They slowly put the tube down my throat. I want to gag, it's so much thicker than my feeding tube. The doctor carefully asks me to swallow so the tube goes through.

"I fucking hated that," I say softly as I approach my mom who has been patiently waiting for me in the waiting room. "Do you ever just wonder what you did wrong to deserve this?" I ask myself and my mother at the same time. "Honey-,"

"No! I'm serious! I can't speak, can't eat. I have a fucking mark that covers half my face!"

"Honey, quiet down, we're in the hospital."

I look around the waiting room, at the people staring at me with their pitiful eyes. I bite my lip and start walking. My mom trails behind me.

The mattress of the hotel room feels hard underneath me. My mom is sound asleep, snoring. I turn on the night light beside my bed. I lay my finger on the sensor and my phone lights up. A familiar place pops up on my TikTok feed. It's my school. There's a girl in it. She has ginger curls. She's laughing with her friend, as she tics. I read the caption, and it simply says, "My favorite ticcy friend." I think to myself: at least I'm not the only one at that shit school with a disability.

Day three.

The nurse hands me the plastic cup of barium. I cringe at only the thought of having to drink this again. It takes me a good few minutes to wash it down. X-ray machine time. I'll be out of here in two hours. Then I'll be on my way home! At last!

Ellie

Miriam and Steph are brabbling about everything and nothing. And honestly, I'm not keeping up. I've been going crazy trying to find this girl. We stand here at the entrance bright and early. So, I can secretly wait for this girl, but it seems she has gone away from existence. Sucked into a black hole. Maybe it was just a dream? No that's stupid. "Hey," I interrupt my friend's very important, air quote that, conversation. "Do you guys know this girl with the feeding tube?"

"Oh, the one with the birthmark?" Steph goes.

I nod. "Yes, her." Thank the lord, she exists, I'm not going crazy. "Oh, that's Jana? I think her name is."

"Hmm," I go. "Okay."

"Why?"

"No reason." Miriam slaps my shoulder. "She's like totally weird." The girls continue their conversation. I try to follow it but it's too much for my brain to handle. I look up again. The heavens must've been listening because there she is. The girl. The girl with the birthmark and feeding tube. I watch her walk past us into the school. I grab my stuff. "I need to go to the toilet."

I run after the girl up the stairs and try to find the courage to talk to her: "Jana?!" The girl comes to a sharp stop and turns around. We stare at each other for a moment. I notice her eyes first, one is blue, and the other one is brown. They're absolutely stunning, even more beautiful than Steph's. "Uhm," I shake my head, then whistle and twitch. "I'm Ellie, I- I just saw you around and I just wanted to say hi?" I cringe at myself. She stares at me. That's all she does, stare. She seems nervous, maybe even more nervous than me. "I- I just wanted to say, ignore Liam, he's an ass."

She nods and smiles shortly. Then she stares again. "Okay," I nod. I throw up my hand. "Bye."

I turn around and curse myself. Stupid, stupid, stupid. She doesn't want to talk to you.

I sit in the quiet classroom. I can feel the electricity surge down my spine. I humph and hit my head. I let out a squeak and throw my head back. I humph again. I'm having a tic attack at school. I go "Whoop!" and "Woah!" and "Hey!" I punch and hit myself. Slam my fists onto the desk. Miriam grabs my hand. The whole class is looking at me. "Ellie, are you okay?" The teacher asks. "Woah! Fuck off! Sluts in slippers!" I punch myself hard in the face. Miriam grabs my other hand and holds them tight. I kick my leg as I lose control of my entire body. "I'm having a tic attack," I manage to say. "Do you want to go to the nurse's office?" I nod as tears start streaming down my face. I get up quickly and make my way out of the classroom with prying eyes.

I walk down the hallways, twitching and ticcing. The few students in the hallways look at me, I can see them judge. They think I'm crazy, the crazy Tourette's girl.

I walk into the nurse's office. Nurse Cooper greets me. "Hi there." But I keep ticcing, I flip her off and make weird noises. "Oh no honey," the chubby black lady says. "You're having a tic attack, sit down." I sit down on the chair and Nurse Cooper gives me a pillow to hold. I rock back and forth, trying to get all the tension out. I smash my head into the pillow repeatedly. Nurse Cooper sits beside me, comforting me as well as she can. Then there's a knock on the door. "Come on in," Cooper says. The door opens with a creak. Then a head pops in. It's Jana. Her eyes lock with mine, but not for long, the blinking tics start up again. "Hi, Jana, you want to take a rest?" She nods shyly and hands Cooper a yellow card that says, "No Spoons Left." Jana walks into the next room, the one where the beds are.

Once the tic attack is over, the only thing that's left of it is small twitches. I yawn and dry my tears. My brain is foggy, and all the energy has been taken from my body. Nurse Cooper hugs me. "You're okay girly." She gets up and walks to her desk. She makes another one of those yellow cards appear. She smiles at me. "I'm allowed to give these to people I think may need them."

I look confused at her and sniff. "It's a Spoonie card." She explains the Spoon Theory to me. "So, this one is for you," she hands me the yellow card. "If you run out of spoons, you show this card to the teacher and you come here to rest and take a break, okay?" I nod. "Do you need a break now?" I nod again, "Yes."

I walk into the room that is attached to the nurse's office. Jana peaks up from underneath the blanket. "Hey," I whisper to her and sit down on the other bed. "So, you're a spoonie too?" I ask her and sniff once again. The tears have left a hard salty crust on my cheeks. She nods. "Are you a sophomore?" She nods again. "Do you, like, not speak?" I ask and chuckle. She seems to think for a moment, then she nods. Embarrassment settles on my face, and I can feel the blood rush in my cheeks. "Sorry, I didn't know you were mute."

She sits up, grabs the tablet she always carries with her, and starts typing, then the monotone AI voice sounds: "I have selective mutism."

I nod. "That's okay."

"You have Tourette's?" The tablet sounds.

I nod again. "Yes, I do."

"I saw it on TikTok."

My eyebrows grow closer together. "What do you mean? I don't post on TikTok."

She types again and the voice sounds: "My favorite ticcy friend."

I bite my lip and feel anger boil up inside me. "Damn! Stephanie!" I jump off the bed and storm out of the nurse's office.

I stomp over to Miriam and Stephanie who are both sitting at one of the outdoor tables. “My favorite ticcy friend!” Steph exclaims. I come to a stop. “Consent is no longer a thing?” Stephanie looks confused at me. My eyes switch between the two girls. “TikTok?!” I exclaim. “It’s just a video,” Steph says and brushes it off. “Not to me! My tics make me feel vulnerable and you took advantage!”

“Woah, can you stop being a fucking dragon?”

I furrow my eyebrows. “Fuck you, Steph.” I turn around and stomp away again. I grab my phone out of my pocket. “Hun?” my mom’s voice sounds after the beeps. “Mom, come pick me up.”

“Why, honey?”

“Had a tic attack.”

“I’ll be on my way.”

I look at the video of my tics. The TikTok video with 21k views. I look at the comments. “I wonder what it’s like dating her, like does she just say what comes to mind?”

“This is fake!! Bad acting!” I scoff. “She can just get away with cussing, I wish I had Tourette’s.”

“OH, I THOUGHT THIS VIDEO WAS A JOKE” I throw my phone across the room. “In what way would it be a joke!” I scream out as tears flood down my face. “How is it a joke?” I whisper to myself. I grab a strand of hair, twist it around my fingers, and pull. I drop the strand of hair on the floor. With a quick woosh, my door flies open. I look at my mom through blurry vision. “Baby, what's wrong?" She rushes over to me and holds me in her arms. "I don't want this anymore!" I sob out. She sees the strand of hair on the floor. "Oh no honey, I thought we were done with that."

I sit in a small office by the window on an uncomfortable plastic chair. I pull the sleeves of my hoodie over my hands and bite my nails as I watch the cars parked in the parking lot down below. I tap each finger to my thumb. Index, middle, ring, pinky. I do it four times. A tall lady walks into the room and sits across from me. "Hey, so you're Ellie?"

I nod and twitch. "I see you used to be in treatment with Marlene?"

I nod again.

"Your mom called us because she's worried about you."

I shrug. "She's just overreacting, I had one bad day."

"But you hurt yourself?"

I readjust myself. "I didn't."

"You pulled your hair out."

"One strand," I throw my hands up and drop them again. "That's still hurting yourself."

My tics flip the psychologist off. "How are you feeling about your tics?"

I take a deep breath and suddenly wish I was Jana. Mute. Maybe then they'd leave me alone. "How are your OCD compulsions?"

I take another deep breath; this is going to be the longest hour of my life.

I walk out of the building. My mom's watches me walk over from behind the wheel. "Hey honey," she says as I get in the car. I stare blankly at her. "So? How did it go?"
"I just want to go home."

Jana

Not a single word. Aloneness – that's what I'd call it. That's what my selective mutism is. I'm isolated, alone. I'm on the outside, looking at the world through a screen. Like I'm watching a movie I'm not a part of. I watch everyone around me experience life as the words freeze up inside me, not willing to come out. Too afraid to speak up or to join a conversation. I am alone. Feeling the anxiety shaking in my chest as I try to get up the courage to speak to someone. I feel like I'm that one kid watching from behind the safety of a window watching the other kids laugh and play but being too afraid to speak three words: can I play? I feel like a fifty-year-old lady, working from inside her cubicle as the world around her drowns out. I live inside a shell. I'm in here but it's really hard to let other people see. I'm not quiet because I'm uncaring, I'm silent because I'm afraid. But oh, how I wish I could just get the words out.

I watch her walk past me. Her twitches are subtle. Something has changed about her. Her aura feels heavy, and her eyes have darkened. She's not okay. I watch her come to a stop. She watches a girl waving her over but ignores it and walks straight inside. The black-haired girl looks confused at the girl sitting beside her. I bet she posted the TikTok. I wish I could stand up, walk over there, and tell them what they did hurt Ellie. But I don't. Because I'm a broken CD, no sound. I take my tablet and write her name as I run after her into the building, trying to catch up with her. Once I'm closely trailing behind her, I press the button. "Ellie," the monotone voice sounds. "Ellie," I try again but the ginger girl keeps walking. Just say it out loud! I can't! I turn up the volume. "Ellie!" the monotone voice sounds once again. She comes to a stop and turns around. Her darkened eyes look at me. I give her a polite smile. "Hey," she tries to say, but her voice cracks. I quickly type and let it play: "Are you okay?"

She shrugs and her eyes glisten with tears. I look down for a minute at my tablet. No. I put it away and grabble my card. I hold it up to her and point. She takes hers and points at it too. I nod. "Let's go," she whispers and together we walk to the nurse's office.

"Ah, my favorite spoonies!" Nurse Cooper welcomes us. I smile at her.

Ellie

I sit on the bed and swing my legs. Jana is lying on the other one biting the chew necklace around her neck.

"Why don't you speak?" I ask her softly. She looks up at me with her heterochromia eyes. She takes her tablet and starts typing. "It's not that easy," it sounds. "To explain?" I ask, and she nods. She types again. "They call me the cow."

I breathe out. "They call me a spaz."

"Do you think I'm ugly?" the voice sounds from the tablet once again. I shake my head. "Not at all." She smiles and her eyes glisten. My tics are calm, but the twitching and jerking still annoy me. Jana puts down her tablet and closes her eyes. I lay myself down, and close mine too. I take a deep breath and say softly: "You don't have to be afraid to talk to me, I just want to let you know that." But the room stays quiet.

The bell sounds loud, and I jot awake. I take a moment to figure out where I am. School. I look at Jana who has also been shaken from her sleep. She looks at me with tired eyes. "So much for rest," I chuckle softly. She gives me a tender smile. I hear the loud chattering of students coming from the hallway, making me want to leave. I look at Jana and she looks at me. "Do you want to go somewhere with me?" Her eyebrows grow closer in confusion. "We're spoonies, we're allowed to leave," I wink at her. She takes her tablet and types. "Where do you want to go?" I shrug and think. I think about how as a child my parents would take me to the park and I'd feed the ducks and frolic in the grass.

"Let's go to the park." Jana's face lights up and she gets onto her feet.

Jana and I run through the park. She doesn't say anything, but I'm not here to force her out of her comfort zone. I run up to a tree and she runs behind me. I laugh and she smiles. The midday sun shines into her eyes, leaving the blue one pale like ice and the other one like honey. I run over to the ducks, and they scurry away quacking. Jana laughs and kneels down beside the lake. Looking at the fish swimming about. I lay myself down flat out on the grass. And smile, letting the warm sunbeams embrace me. I can feel Jana's presence beside me. I open a single eye and look at her. She's lying on her stomach, resting on her elbows. She smiles at me. I want to tell her how beautiful she is. Because I know how insecure she is about that birthmark. But it makes her unique. It makes her, *her*. I want to tell her that her beauty doesn't scare me. But instead, I laugh and ask: "Are you feeling better?" She nods and turns onto her back. She squints her eyes at the bright sky and then closes them, and so do I. And once again, I let the warmth of the sun kiss my skin.

Jana

I walk into the kitchen with the brightest smile on my face. My mom is cooking, and it smells heavenly. "So," she starts, "Who is this girl you hung out with?" I tilt my head at her. "Ellie," I say softly. "Is she nice?"

"Yes," I twirl. "Have you talked to her?"
"Nope," I simply say. "And here's the thing, she doesn't force me to either."
"Will you one day speak to her?"
I shrug. "Maybe."
"Do you want to?"
I smile at my mother. "Of course, I do."

I hold my head above the toilet, getting ready to throw up my mom's delicious dinner. The nausea is terrible, it feels like my soul is leaving my body. The nausea is ten times worse than the actual throwing up. And there it is. I hate the sound of it splashing into the toilet. But it's not done yet. I throw up some more.

I scroll through my TikTok likes, hoping the video got taken down. I scroll and scroll and then, there it is "video no longer available." I smile. I guess she came to her senses.

Ellie

I flush the toilet and make my way to the sink. I turn on the water and put soap on my hands and start washing. *Wash three times. You have to wash them three times.* I turn off the faucet and stand there for a moment. *Three times.* I wash them again, and once again. I turn off the faucet again. *No there are germs on my hands, I have to wash them again.* I place my hands on the sink and take a deep breath. Once again.

I walk into my room and close the door behind me. *Tap the wall with each one of your fingers.* I tap my thumb, index, middle, ring, and pinky. *Again*. Thumb, index, *no you tapped it too long!* Thumb, index, middle, ring, pinky. Done.

I take my rainbow medicine box and pour my Friday night medication onto my desk. *Check them three times, otherwise, you'll die*. I check them once, twice, and three times.

I lay in my bed, staring at the ceiling above. My head is tired, but my body isn't. *Tap the wall seven times*. I tap the wall seven times. *Now knock four times.* I knock four times. My mind is quiet, I close my eyes.

November

Ellie

“I am Mrs. Glasgow. I’m your substitute teacher for now, whilst your teacher is on pregnancy leave,” the short chubby older lady goes. Her hair has gone completely grey, and her skin is old of age. I humph once and then whistle. I look at Miriam and Steph sitting at the front of the class. I will not talk to them unless they decide to apologize for what they did. I go “Woah” and whistle again. “Okay, keep it down,” the old lady says annoyed. But there we go again “c-c-cunt!” my tics yell very loud. The old lady gives me a death stare. “Do you think you’re the class clown or something? I will not tolerate this kind of behavior!” My heart pounds loudly in my chest. “I’m sorry, I have a disability.”

“So? Does that mean you get to yell obscenities? Do you think you’re *special*?”

“No,” I stutter, “I- I have Tourette’s, I can’t help it, fuck!”

“Well try, because I will not tolerate a distraction like that!”

“I literally cannot control it.”

“Then get out of my class.” I stare at her for a moment unable to find a response to that. “Go on, out!” I scoff. “You can’t just throw me out. The Americans with Disabilities Act prohibits it!”

"This is my classroom and you're disturbing it. If you only have one leg, you can't go to the dance academy!" I scoff and stand up, grabbing my stuff and leaving. I will not be treated unfairly like this!

I lay on one of the beds in the nurse's office. Fidgeting with my Sunflower Lanyard. I read the short sentence over and over again. "I have Tourette's" but oh God, how I wish I didn't.

Jana

I knock on the door. My yellow card in hand. I can hear Nurse Cooper's faint voice saying "Come in." I carefully open the door and hold up my Spoonie Card. "Ah," she goes. "Good you're here, you can keep your friend a bit of company." *Ellie?* I smile and nod. I walk into the small room and watch Ellie look up from her lanyard. She smiles. "Hey." I wave my hand at her and scurry over to the other bed to take a seat. I watch her darkened eyes before grabbing my tablet. I start typing and then press the button. "Are you okay?"

She looks at me for a moment and then shakes her head. I type again. "What's wrong?"

"I got kicked out of class by our substitute teacher." I frown at her and type. "Is that even allowed?"

Ellie lets out a painful chuckle. "No, it's not." I hesitate for a moment and then stand up. I walk over to the beautiful girl and sit down beside her, throwing my arm over her shoulder and letting her lean onto me. We sit like that for a while. All I can think about is that I want to speak, I want to let words out and tell Ellie it'll be okay and that we're going to get through this. But instead, I sit in silence, because even though my lips can part, I have no words.

She sits up straight again and softly smiles at me. "Thank you for being there for me," she says quietly. I nod and grab my tablet. I type and hesitate for a moment but then click the button anyway. I look her in the eyes as the device speaks for me. "You make me happy, Ellie. Nothing ever makes me happy."

Her eyes glisten with tears and she chuckles. "You make me happy too."

We're sitting on the grass. Ellie keeps letting her hand stroke the green leaves as we both sit in silence. I take my tablet and type. "I'm getting a GJ-tube soon."

Ellie looks up at me. "In your stomach?"

I nod and type. "I hate my NJ-tube."

"Why?"

"It makes me ugly."

"It really doesn't," Ellie tries to assure me. "You're the absolute opposite of ugly."

I smile and can feel the blood rush going down my cheeks. I type again. "I want you to be there."

"Where?"

"When I get my GJ-tube." Ellie smiles at me and nods. "If you want me to be there, I'll be there." I open my mouth. Just speak the two words. That's what I tell myself. I try to push them out, past my lips. But I can't. I grab my tablet and type again. "Thank you."

Ellie

"Ellie!" I hear my mother yell from downstairs. I groan and put down the pen I was doing my homework with. "There's someone here for you!" My eyebrows furrow, who in the hell? I get up from behind my messy desk and make my way downstairs. I come to a sharp stop as I see Miriam and Stephanie standing in our living room. "Look!" Mai goes. "Your friends are here!" I smile shortly at my little sister. "What are you doing here?" I ask, maybe slightly annoyed. "You can't ignore us forever," Steph shrugs. "We're your friends."

"Friends don't do what you did Steph."

"I meant no harm!" she defends herself.

"Well, you did! Did you see those comments?!"

Miriam shyly looks at me from behind the tall girl. "We're sorry Ellie, we really are."

"Are you now?" I say annoyed.

"Yes!" Stephanie exclaims. "I took the video down."

"Please Ellie, we love you, please forgive us."

"Forgive them!" My little sister jumps up and down.

"I'll think about it," I say shortly before turning around and disappearing up the stairs again. I lean my back against the wall waiting for the front door to close again and only then do I let out a deep breath.

“Do we have everything?” I ask as I put the last things in Jana’s rainbow tote bag. It takes a while for her to type before the tablet goes. “I think we do.”

I look around her room one more time. There are so many fake vines that make the room look like a fairy’s hideout. On the door, there’s a quote that reads “Every pain has a purpose.” From the stand of her feeding tube is a garland of hospital tags. “Thank you for being here,” the monotone voice of the tablet sounds. I smile at the girl. “No problem.”

“Let’s go girls!” Jana’s mom sounds from downstairs. Today Jana’s NJ-Tube is getting replaced by a GJ-Tube.

Jana

I walk out of the little hospital bathroom that’s attached to my little hospital room. The grippy socks feel soft around my feet. My mom and Ellie are laughing and making conversation. I walk over to the bed and take a seat. “Are you ready?” my mom asks me, I nod. I had hoped I would be able to speak to Ellie if my mom was around, but quite the opposite happened. I can’t even speak to my mom. The nurse and doctor walk in. “Let’s get you all ready,” the tall man says. They start by hooking me to all the monitors so they can keep a close eye on my blood pressure, oxygen levels, and heart rate. Next thing, they put in an intravenous line. “I’m going to take your NJ-tube out now.” The young nurse tells me. She seems nervous. I nod and smile. Now we wait for the surgery.

They roll me away. I hold my hand out to Ellie. She takes it for a split second. Then I'm out of the room and off to the operating room.

The first thing I notice as I'm waking is how hot and humid it is. My body is sticky all over, especially under the covers. There's a stinging sensation, like sweat on a cut, on my stomach. I slowly open my eyes, letting them adjust to the bright light of day. I try to move, but my body is feeling stiff, and heat and I never get along. My mind is fuzzy at first, but then, I start remembering things. I'm in a hospital. I look to my side. My mom jumps up. "There you are!" she smiles softly. "The surgery went well," she winks at me. I look around but something is missing. "Where's Ellie?"

"She went outside for a moment, to get some fresh air, she'll be back soon."

I nod sleepily. I can hear the door open and quickly open my eyes, hoping to see Ellie, instead, the young nurse from earlier walks in. She checks all the machines and then turns to me. "How is the pain?" I shrug. "Not too bad." She smiles, "Good, that means the painkillers are doing their job."

"You're awake!" a familiar voice sounds from behind the nurse. I smile at Ellie rushing over to me. She plops down on my bed, and I blink sleepily. "You tired?" Ellie asks.

Ellie

Jana slowly nods and lets out a scratchy "Yeah." I blink once and watch Jana fall back into a slumber. I look up at her mother in disbelief. She smiles at me and taps her cheek with her index finger. "She hasn't said a word to anyone except me for years." I need to let that sink in for a moment.

It took a while but finally, Jana lets out a groan. She hisses and then continues to bite her teeth. I can't imagine how painful and sore her stomach must be. Her heterochromia eyes meet mine; she lets out a short smile. I smile back. I want to lay my head on her shoulder, I want her to hold me and never let me go. But she probably doesn't. What am I thinking? She grabs her tablet and starts typing, the monotone voice sounds: "Thank you for being here with me, you truly are my only friend."

I smile softly, then whistle and jerk my neck. I grab her hand and lay my head beside her. "Thank you for being there for me Jana, for understanding."

"Thank *you*," she says, and I jerk up. She smiles at me with tears trickling down her face. She repeats herself: "Thank you."

I stomp my way over to the two girls I call my friends. Stephanie is lying with her head on Miriam's lap. Miriam spots me and nudges Steph who then proceeds to also look at me and sits herself up. "Where were you? We've been trying to contact you all weekend!" Steph exclaims. I take a deep breath and look at the girl with pitch-black hair. "I was with Jana."

"Jana?" Miriam asks.

"Birthmark girl?" Stephanie asks in a high-pitched voice. I angry-frown at her. "She's my friend," I say annoyed. "Friend?" Steph scoffs. "She doesn't even talk." I bite my lip and look up to the heavens for a second. "Okay," I start. "I came here to accept the apology, but you just screwed things up a second time." I take a deep breath and turn around. "No! Wait!" Steph yells. I come to a sharp stop and do a one-eighty. "I'm sorry," I look at her pale blue eyes. She sighs. "I'm sorry, okay? I didn't think it was a big deal. T-The video I mean," she stutters. I look behind her at Miriam who is looking at me through sheepish eyes. "I took it down."

"Thank you," I say softly.

"Can we now please stop this stupid fight?" Miriam's soft voice sounds.

Steph looks at me and smiles kindly. "Once your friend over there stops being an asshole." I spit at her.

Jana

My mom walks into my room as I sleepily scroll through my phone. I look up, her face is twisted. I already know what that means. "Bad news," she goes, I knew it. "We need to go to the emergency room." I sigh and drop my head back. "Seriously?" She nods shyly. "Stupid GJ-tube," I mutter from underneath my breath.

Yesterday evening I noticed a black spot at the top of my GJ-tube, possibly mold. And that is never good. I stayed home because my mom had to contact my doctor about this issue. What should've been a normal day will be another day spent in a hospital. As I said. It really is my second home.

The car shudders underneath me as we drive onto the hospital's parking lot, looking out the window as my mom finds a spot. The midday sun is shining bright, but the temperatures have been dropping. I'm not looking forward to getting out and into the cold. I want to sit here in the warm car as the air conditioning heats the air. But alas, the car shudders once more before going dead. Let's do this.

After an hour in the waiting room of the very busy emergency department, we were finally guided to my room. I feel cold in this pale blue hospital gown and nestle myself in the bed. I pull the heavy covers over my entire body, leaving nothing out but my face. I shiver once. "Are you cold?" my mom asks. I nod. "Yeah, it's fucking freezing."

The nurse enters the room in blue scrubs, po-faced, serious, washing her hands at the sink. When she turns to me her face softens into a smile and she introduces herself before asking what had brought me to the hospital. I look over at my mom to say the words for me. She listens to my mom explain while taking my pulse. Then she's gone. Po-faced again, washing hands, writing on a folder outside the door. So, this is my nurse for the day, I sigh and roll toward my mom, raising my eyebrows, I've had worse. At least this one tried to be nice.

The bored-looking nurse from earlier guides me through the hallways. The hallway has as much personality as the rest of the hospital. The floor is slate grey, and the walls dove. Above, the ceiling is made from those polystyrene squares laid on a grid-like frame. The light is too bright for my eyes, enough perhaps to bring on one of my migraines. Above every door I pass is a large plastic sign, dark with white lettering- no fancy fonts, just bold and all-caps. Finally, the plastic sign that reads "Radiology" appears. Arrived at destination.

The doctor walks in with a big smile which indicates it is most likely good news. It's not one of those pitiful I'm-going-to-give-you-bad-news kind of smiles. The bored nurse stands behind him. "Good news," he starts. "The mold in your tube has not infected your stomach. Less good news, our friendly nurse here," he points to the woman behind him. I want to scoff but swallow it down. "Is going to have to replace your tube." I simply nod.

Ellie

I knock on the green door of the small city row house. I've been trying to contact Jana all day. She didn't show up at school. It takes a few seconds before the door opens. Jana's mother appears and smiles politely at me. "Hey, Ellie, what brings you here?"

"Is Jana okay? She didn't show up to school."

Her mom's eyes soften. "We had to go to the emergency room. She's upstairs in her room, she's a bit tired."

"Emergency room?" I say slightly worried.

"Oh, it's nothing. You should go to her, I think she can benefit from some cheering up," her mother winks.

Jana

I'm chewing on my chew necklace as I can hear my door softly creak. I sigh softly, expecting to see my mother but when I look up, I see Ellie's face appear. "Hey," she says softly. I force myself into a sitting position and wave my hand at her as my chest flutters. I talked to her, and I said the words, yet I'm not capable of doing it again.

Ellie lays on my bed, her head over the edge, her ginger hair almost reaching the floor. I could spend all day with Ellie: chatting, venting, laughing. She doesn't care that my only way of communicating is via tablet. The house is a mess but, it doesn't matter, Ellie doesn't care. For several sweet hours, I won't have to hide behind a mask, not of happiness, not of coping. I can be honest without fear of judgment. Ellie is my best friend. And I haven't had a friend for years. Though I would be lying if I said I don't long for more.

December

Ellie

There's loud music playing through the city's plaza. The Christmas market is up and running. Jana is smiling beside me, clinging to my arm, and pointing around. She's quite the Christmas spirit. The evening sky has darkened into blue. The lights are flickering brightly all over. The sound of people chattering fills my ears. A group of kids runs past us bumping their way through the crowd. The smell of sugar waffles and eggnog infiltrates my nostrils, the air is more delicious than any flavor could ever be. Jana drags my attention to the big carousel. Colored flashing lights illuminate the faces of the laughing children going up and down on their fake horses. It plays loud music, *Silent Night*, over and over again.

Jana confidently skates around the ice ring. I, on the other hand, am clutching tightly to the edge, my legs wobbly underneath me. The ice has a diamond glow, reflecting the bright white fairy lights all around. She waves me over again. She chuckles, probably because of the horror on my face. I've never liked ice skating.

"I would also like a sugar waffle," Jana's tablet sounds as the waiter writes down our order. Jana looks at me and then starts typing again. “I better not throw up. Stupid gastroparesis.”

I chuckle. “You’ll be fine.” She smiles softly at me. We both shift our attention to the big Ferris wheel, in all its glory and flashing lights. I share a look with Jana, her eyebrows go up. I tilt my head, trying to convince her without words. She sighs and smiles, “Fine,” she says softly. I smile brightly. Her voice still sends butterflies through my stomach.

My eyes widen. The Ferris wheel comes to a stop. I look over to Jana. Her heterochromia eyes lock with mine. “Why did we stop?” I ask her, and she shrugs. “Are we meant to stop?” I look down at the faraway ground. “We’re supposed to be moving.”

“Oh, this is bad,” Jana’s tablet says. I look into her eyes. “We’ll be fine,” I try to shrug it off. “You’re scared,” the tablet says. I grind my teeth; she sees right through me. “Okay, so I’m not fine,” I rattle. I look around nervously. I hear Jana chuckle. I look at her. “What? What!?” She types quickly, “You wanted to go on the Ferris Wheel.”

I grind my teeth. I am scared of heights, why did I do this? There’s a soft touch on my hand. My head turns quickly. I watch Jana intertwine our hands. My heart pounds in my chest. I hesitate before looking up at her. I take in her beautiful features once more. Her eyes, her hair, her face. It's that she cares so very much about others that makes her so beautiful to me. That she sees my beauty, that she shows how special I am, that's what's got me for life. She isn't just beautiful, she makes the space around her beautiful too, she affects others and brings their beauty out of them. And she does it with ease. It is who she is. She is a flower that makes others bloom, that makes me bloom.

The cart shudders underneath us as it goes back into motion. She nudges me and chuckles. "There, we're going again." I smile brightly at her, "Your voice is beautiful." She chuckles. "I saved it for you," her eyes sparkle. I can feel the bright smile on my face, and the muscles in the corners of my mouth are tense. "For me?" I say through my stupid smile. "For you."

I lean my head on her shoulder. "Ellie?" her soft voice sounds. "Yeah?" I look up at her. She opens her mouth to speak, but the words seem to be stuck. I give her a moment, maybe she wants to grab her tablet. "Ellie..." she goes again. I wait patiently. She lifts her hand to my cheek. "Thank you," she whispers. Then she leans in, and my eyes widen for a second as her lips meet mine. At first, there's tension but then I release it all as I sink into her. Her lips taste like honey and apple pie baked just right. She makes me feel at home.

I sit at the back of the class. I yawn in boredom and then tic once. I watch Miriam and Stephanie in the front, laughing together. Once our teacher is done writing on the smart board, he turns around to look at us. "So!" He goes loudly, getting our attention. "In today's *Life Lesson* class, we're going to talk about friendship." He eyes over the class, and we all look bored. "One of you, can you tell me what you need in a friendship and what you don't want." He eyes us over again. Stephanie abruptly stands up, making me jump up a bit. "What I need in a friendship, is someone that spends time with you. What I really don't need-," she looks at me. "Is someone that will abandon me." I look at her pale blue eyes. I bite the inside of my cheek. Fuck this. I stand up as well. "You know what I would want in a friendship? Consent. What don't I need?" My furious eyes go to her. "Someone that takes advantage of me." Stephanie rolls her eyes and sits back down. "Shut up, Spaz," she goes. My heart drops in my chest. I look at Miriam who is shyly hiding her face. "Do you even care about me?" I exclaim. "Okay, okay, settle down," the teacher demands me, but I don't. "Do you actually like me, or do you just think I'm interesting because I have a disability?" Steph turns around to look at me. "Do you really care, or do you just want to post videos of my Tourette's on TikTok hoping it'll go viral so you can get likes?"

"Oh, shut up!" Steph yells at me. I bite my lip until it bleeds. My blood is boiling. I grab my stuff and head for the door. "Hey! Where are you going?" The teacher yells after me. I flash him my yellow spoonie card before storming out the door.

I lay down on the bed in the nurse's office. Tears trickle down my face. The weight of the blankets is holding me down. They twist around my infinitely heavy body. What am I supposed to do? Tell her it's all right? Tell her that what she did was fine? Because that's what I'd be doing if I forgave her. I can't forgive her. Cut me some slack here. For all my teenage years I've been afraid to be judged. Judged for the person I am. I thought I found some good friends but then they go and do me wrong. I roll over onto my side and sniff, trying to stop the tears from leaking out. I close my eyes, trying to fall into slumber. Because that's the only way to stop hurting.

My alarm sounds loud. It's another day. I lay my finger on the screen and the ringing stops. The world around me is quiet. I lay numb. Like always it crept up on me slowly. You begin struggling with the little things, but you choose to ignore them and go on with your days like normal. You shrug it off, you're just having a bad day. But it's always there, in the back of your mind. So, you put on this social mask, you don't let anyone see. You just continue on because that's what others do. I throw off the blanket and sit up, letting my feet touch the cold floor of my messy room. There's a soft knock on my door. I sleepily turn my head. My mom's face pops up from behind it. "It's almost time for school," she says. I blink once and blankly stare. I can't do it. "Are you okay, honey?" she asks. I run my hand through my hair and shrug. Why would I keep on trying if nothing makes me happy anymore? My mom slowly walks over to me and sits down, putting her arm over my shoulder. I lean into her as the sadness inside me grows. I grab her sweater and hold it tightly as the tears finally make their way down my face. “How about you stay home today?” her worried voice sounds. I sob and take a deep breath. “Yes, please.”

My face is squished into the pillow, my eyelids are heavy. I try to concentrate on the movie, but my mind is blank. Tears still slowly trickle down my face. It seems like I’ll never stop. Day after day, I lay here. I’m still wearing the same blue sweater I wore the first day I stayed home. How long ago was that even? I don’t remember. All the days are merging and I’m in a constant state of sadness. I know my mom is getting worried. She keeps walking into the living room every half an hour. I try to not look at her because when I do, I can see the worry on her face. She doesn’t want her little girl to be hurt. I can see my phone ringing every once in a while. My mom will walk into the living room, “Shouldn’t you get that?” I shrug, I know who it is, Jana. I don’t want to be a burden to her. I’ve become so used to being in this state that I’ve forgotten when it started. I wish I could tell someone and ask for help, but I don’t want to be burdensome. After all, I’m already a waste of space. I can’t tell anyone because, after all, my life hasn’t completely fallen apart yet, so why would anyone believe I’m struggling?

"Honey, come on," my mom softly says. "We need to get you washed someday." I blink once. "I'm too tired."

"Honey, you haven't left the couch in days."

I sit in the bathtub, hugging myself closely. Soft sobs escape my mouth. The warm water embraces my stone-cold body. My mom shampoos my hair as I just continue crying. Some things might seem obvious and easy to you. Like brushing your teeth and combing your hair. But right now, for me, those things are insurmountable tasks.

I hug my washed body close. I'm on the couch again. My purple sweater feels comfortable. I readjust my body and blankly stare at the TV screen again.

Jana

My bare hands are in the pockets of my winter jacket in hopes of keeping them warm but the cold seeps through the fabric. My body shivers and the wind cuts my face. My teeth clatter. It's the beginning of winter but it sure is freezing cold already. The sky above me is as white as can be. I wiggle my toes in my shoes, making sure they haven't frozen off yet. I need to get to Ellie's house. I've been trying to contact her for one and a half weeks now, getting increasingly more worried over the unanswered texts and call attempts. Ellie's mother contacted me a few days ago, letting me know she was still alive, just not doing so well. So here I am, school just ended and I'm making my way to her house.

My warm lungs fill with cold air and as I release it again there's a cloud of smoke. All that's missing is snow.

I come to a stop in front of the house. The wind still wraps around me as I keep shivering. I pull my hand out of my pocket, making it even colder than before. My fingers have started turning red. I knock softly and quickly hide my hand in the pocket of my jacket again. It doesn't take long before the door opens, and a kind-looking woman greets me. Once I'm inside there's a relief. The warm air comforts my cold ears, and I can finally take my hands out of my pockets. The house smells like lavender. I follow the woman through the house.

The voices on the TV get clear as I enter the living room. I can see Ellie's ginger hair. Her body is under a thick fluffy blanket. I look at her lying still, sound asleep. Her mother whispers to me. "You can wake her up if you want." I smile and go: "It's okay, I'll just wait." Her mother smiles politely before disappearing into the next room.

Ellie

I give myself a moment to shed the sleep from my brain. Half-awake is my favorite state of being. My brain is in that purgatory state, where I'm awake and living, but still asleep to enjoy peace of mind. "Hey," a soft voice sounds and suddenly I'm out of that state. My eyes scan the room until they fall on a familiar face. I sit up abruptly. “Jana?” my voice cracks. She smiles a painful smile. “What are you doing here?”

She shrugs. “Just checking up on you.”

“Why didn’t you tell me?” her soft voice goes.

“I didn’t want to be a burden.”

“You could never ever, be a burden to me.”

I shrug. “I feel like I’m a burden to everyone.”

“What happened?” her worried voice sounds again. I shrug. “Is it because of that Stephanie girl?”

“No.” I simply say.

“Then why?”

I bite my lip. “Sometimes there is no ‘why’.”

Then it goes quiet. I tap each of my fingers to my thumb. Jana speaks again: “Are you up to going to the Snow Ball?” it’s quiet again. I look up at her. At her heterochromia eyes. I bite my lip. “Not really,” my voice cracks. She smiles shortly. “Not even with me?” My heart drops in my chest. Did she really just ask me to go to the Snow Ball with her?

Jana

I can see her eyes widen at my question. My heart is pounding in my chest, but I won’t let her notice. I want to talk to her, but every time I speak my heart rate spikes. I really like this girl and I don’t want to only communicate through my tablet. I bite the inside of my cheek. Why is she quiet? *Stupid me, why would she want to go with you?* My thoughts mock me. I open my mouth and take a deep breath. “You’re allowed to say ‘no.’ If you don’t want to go with me that’s fine.” Her eyes shift from me to the floor a few times. She pinches her eyes closed. “Jana-,” she starts. “I would love to go with you.” I smile for a second. “But I don’t know if I’m up to a big social event.” I bite my lip. “Of course.”

“Can I think about it?” she says shyly.

“Definitely, of course, you can.” I smile at her, hoping to get one back, but instead, she stares at the floor. She’s hurting.

I just throw everything in the shopping cart, my mom tracing behind me. I asked Ellie’s mother what she enjoys doing. We want to get her off of that couch, we want to see her smile again. Her mother had said Ellie has always loved baking but doesn’t do it quite often because of her tics. So, I just throw everything in the cart, baking powder, food colorings, ready-to-make boxes of brownie ingredients. I will try with all my might to get her smile back.

I basically drag Ellie to her kitchen. The tiles on the wall are a very light pink and the stove is one that runs on gas rather than electricity. She sighed and muttered, but I had told her that living on the couch for even a day longer would be much worse than baking with me.

She takes a moment to stare at everything I bought. She fills her cheeks with air before letting it out in a sigh.

"Muffins?" she asks shyly. I smile and nod. "Penis!" her tics yell out. "Nick's got a big dick!" the tics continue. "Muffins it is!" I yell out. Talking to Ellie has become so easy. I never thought I'd be able to talk to anyone ever. She helped me, so I will help her.

Ellie grabs the flour and whistles once. She shrugs her shoulders and flour flies everywhere. She takes a deep breath, but I can't help but smile. She looks at me annoyed. I chuckle softly and grab the bag of flour from her. "It's fine!" I tell her. "Your mom will clean up."

"Will I now?" her mom says from behind us. Ellie looks up at her mom and laughs softly. My heart flutters. There it is! Her smile!

"Ay cunt!" she yells out and clicks her tongue. The mess we've made is worse than if a nuclear bomb hit our country right now.

"Not the eggs!" Ellie yells out and laughs hysterically. "You don't want to know what happens when I hold eggs!"

I chuckle, egg in hand. "Well, now I do."

I hold out the egg to her, her tics flap her arms around. She leans closer to the egg and goes "Tweet, tweet!" She dares to grab the egg, but her tics make her shake the egg vigorously. She holds it by her mouth and goes "Tweet, tweet," again. Then it catapults through the kitchen and cracks on the pink tile. Air flies out of my lungs as I burst out laughing. Ellie pouts her mouth through chuckles. She suddenly grabs another egg and smashes it on her forehead. She gasps loudly but I just laugh even more.

Ellie carefully watches me put the hot oven plate on the countertop. Smelling of chocolate and sweetness. She smiles triumphantly at our concoction. "I'll spit on your biscuits!" her tics go. She looks at me and yes, there it is, she has found her smile again.

I walk into the living room. My clothes are covered in flour. My mom looks up at me from her book. "How did it go?"

I smile brightly. "Safe to say she's found her smile again."

"Are you taking her to the Snow Ball?"

I shrug. "She isn't up to it, but that's okay, all I wanted was to see her smile again."

"Are you going to go with someone else?"

I tilt my head. "No. I couldn't. If I can't go with Ellie, I'm not going at all."

Ellie

"There are so many parts!" I go as my mom, and I are setting up the Christmas tree. I've got some kind of branch in my hand. I've always hated our artificial Christmas tree. I'd much rather have a real one.

The plastic-smelling Christmas tree is in the corner of our living room, right next to the window. My mom hands me a box of Christmas ornaments but regrets it quickly as my tics turn it upside down, making them all clatter onto the floor, some break. My mom holds her hands at the side of her face. I grind my teeth and chuckle. “Sorry.” I notice some of the ornaments have found their way into the tree during the avalanche of my tics. I gasp and point, and my mom starts laughing.

I tiredly lay on the couch like a potato sack. *Home Alone* is playing on the TV. My mom has gone to get my little sister Mai from school; my dad can also get home from work at any minute.

Mai gets way too excited about the tree and all its flashing lights. She jumps around and points and laughs. My dad walks in shortly after. Admiring the tree as well. He looks at me and winks. “Looks good.”

“But some ornaments didn’t quite get through Tourette’s in one piece.” My mom jokes. I chuckle and so does my dad.

January

Jana

Do you ever wonder how a person with gastroparesis lives? How do they go through their day? What are they limited to? Well, let me take you with me for a day.

Sunday, January 1st, 2023.

I sit on the cold tiles of the bathroom. It's two thirty in the morning. My elbow is leaning on the toilet seat. So far, I've thrown up twice.

I crawl into a fetal position. The birds have started chirping outside and the light of day slowly creeps up on me. My stomach hurts. I barely had any sleep.

Sadly, I can't stay in bed all day.

Same routine every morning:
Flush tube.
Take off the extension and rinse it out.
Take oral medication.
Use a cotton swab to clean around the tube.
Hook myself back up to my feeds.

It's one of those days. One of the days when there's no school, thank the Lord. No hospital visits, screenings, scans, or doctors. I should be happy about that, but I'm not, because it means I have an entire day of doing nothing. All my life is hospitals and scans. So, what do I do on days without them?

Bed
Couch
Laptop
Draw a bit.
Bed
Couch

Let's just say living with chronic illness isn't ideal.

Ellie

I walk over the schoolyard. My hands are freezing cold as the winter wind washes away their warmth. It's school again, winter break has officially come to an end. I hurry inside.

I no longer look in their direction when I walk into class. It's weird how quickly you can become strangers again. Stephanie and Miriam laugh. I guess they don't need me anymore if they ever even did.

"It's a support group," my mom says from behind the steering wheel. Her eyes are soft, but her hands clutch the steering wheel tight, making the veins in her hands more prominent. I wonder who's more nervous, me or her. I stare at the church in front of me. It has an enormous cross mounted onto the highest part of the building. Below it, situated on a small arch, is a pearly white Mother Maria statue. The windows are tall and big, tinted glass in reds, greens, and blues. “Mom, this is a church,” I say flat-out.

“Give it a chance honey, you need to connect with other people with Tourette’s.”

“Or do you just need other parents with children with Tourette’s?” I jokingly mock her, tilting my head and smirking. She gives me a side eye with a smile. Pleading me without words. “Fine, we’ll go in,” I say defeated, slapping my hands onto my thighs.

“Wanker! Wanker!” is the first thing I hear when I enter through the door. My mom trails behind me. I whistle once. “Tits and dicks!” a girl in a forest green sweater goes before she twitches her neck, making me twitch mine. I look around at all these teenagers, all having Tourette’s yet all having completely different tics. There are about three different whistles, all in a different rhythm and tone. My mom lays her hands on my shoulders, I can feel the pressure of her wedding ring through my black turtleneck. She nudges me forward and I dare to take a few more steps into the room. The room is enormous, and the ceiling is tall and goes into a pointed center. Big biblical paintings stretch out over every arch of the ceiling. One of them has a big grass field with multiple thin wooden crosses on them. I almost want to cringe. Parents are chatting with each other while the kids kind of shyly stay away from one another holding dark blue plastic cups with juice in them. “Hi, there!” a young chubby lady approaches us. I whistle flip her off and go “Nick’s got a big dick!” She doesn’t bat an eye, no reaction, no nothing. I almost want to hug her and tell her how much I appreciate it. She has a short golden blonde bob. “Who are you?” she asks me with a kind smile showing perfect white teeth. “Ellie,” I simply go. She scans the papers in her hands. “Right gotcha, you can go mingle, we’re still waiting for a few more people,” she smiles and slightly leans forward before turning around and walking away.

I sit down on one of the chairs that form a circle in the middle of the big church room. They’re an ugly orange and feel uncomfortable below my butt. There’s only one other girl already on the chairs, she looks small and fragile, hiding behind her long auburn hair. She twitches every few seconds and pops her mouth but never looks up.

“I get a lot that people ask me why my eyes keep twitching,” a boy with a shaven head explains to the group. He throws his head back before continuing to speak. “Or they’ll ask me if I can just stop moving my leg.” Whistle, mouth pop, blink, which makes me humph, clap, and jerk. Which then causes a girl with bright red hair to go “wow.”

"It's just hard to explain to them I can't control it," he finishes.

"And if you do explain and say you have Tourette's, (woah), Tourette's Syndrome they tell you that, you're (a whore), you're faking," the girl with the red hair says. Her hair is the brightest red ever to red and I want to applaud her for what she's wearing. Big chunky black boots. A dark red plaid skirt and a Slipknot T-shirt. Around her neck is an entire collection of chains, thick and thin, accompanied by a spikey chocker. That's one way to enter a church, I'm surprised she didn't combust into flames when walking in. I stay quiet and move my gaze to the next person talking. "I had people tell me that I had to discipline Jason," a lady with a black pixie cut says as she lays her hand on her son's shoulder. "That he was doing it to be disrespectful or that Tourette's wasn't a real thing, and it was hard on me, but mostly on Jason." Jason barks twice.

"When I was first diagnosed, I was out of school for weeks. My tics were so severe that they didn't know what to do with them at school, cunt! And I had to actually-," Clap, clap, clap. Someone whistles, another one barks, and I jerk and humph. "I had to double my year and I'm almost going to graduate from high school soon and I don't know what I'll do after that."

"Are you scared you won't get a job?" The lady that is hosting this group asks the boy, whose name I think is Josh. He nods and clicks his tongue a few times.

“My tics can be pretty harmful, I mean I’ve had many, (dicks!) Injuries because of them,” a tall lean girl gives her part. Then it falls quiet. The lady looks at the fragile young girl, the one with the Auburn hair. “What about you Emily?” she asks. But Emily just hides behind her hair. Her mom squeezes her thigh, but Emily doesn’t want to talk. She takes a deep breath and lets it out in a shaky breath. The lady then fixes her eyes on me and my heart rate spikes. I can feel my eyes widen for a second and I hope no one noticed. “What about Ellie?” she smiles. I whistle and humph and take a second to calm myself done. I also take a shaky breath and muster up the courage to speak my part. “I think people don’t see you as a person,” I say so softly I doubt anyone can understand, yet they all listen. “My friend filmed my tics to post them on social media for likes,” I rattle out.

“Yeah, I’ve had people trying to befriend me simply because I have Tourette’s,” Jason says. I smile at him. They *do* understand.

Jana

I shuffle my hands underneath my butt. There’s pressure on my knuckles from where the pale blue chair presses onto them. I clear my throat as I wait for Ms. Laurence to get her notepad and pen. She sits down on the chair across from me and lets out a small humph as she settles down. “So, Jana, how have you been doing?”

I shrug, take my hands out from underneath me, and start fidgeting with the purple rubber case around my tablet. I somehow cracked the screen. "I noticed you made a friend."

I shrug again. "Can you please communicate with me through your tablet?"

I grind my teeth and never look up at her. My eyes shift to the cracks in my tablet, and I start tracing them with my finger. "Jana?"

I take a deep shaky breath before unlocking my tablet. I type her name and the monotone voice goes: "Ellie."

"Yes," Miss Laurence goes. "Ellie, that's your friend, right?"

I nod. "Do you talk to her?"

I nod again. I can see you shift yourself from the corners of my eyes. "That's great Jana!" she says in a high-pitched voice. A smile creeps up on me, but I push it down. I wave a strand of hair from my vision and shift my gaze to the parking lot below. "I'm really proud of you, Jana," she continues. I look her in the eyes. Smile shortly and speak the words: "Thank you." She blinks twice and sits up a bit straighter before a smile spreads on her face. "Now, that's a lot of progress!" I chuckle.

February

Ellie

It's my birthday.

I open the blinds and let the sun shine through the suncatchers on my window. I admire the rainbows cast all around my room. Today I turn fifteen.

The steps of our stairs creak below my feet as I make my way downstairs. My arms swing around. The first thing I notice is the flags hanging in the living room archway. Bright and purple, with the number fifteen in shining golden letters. I smile stupidly and shake my head. As I walk into the living room there are tons of balloons, also purple. Doing a little dance as they bob around. I get the urge to cut the strings and watch them float up to the ceiling like I did when I was a kid. I'd jump and try to grasp the strings, once I did, I'd pull them down and let them go again, watching them slowly float up again. I chuckle as I make my way into the dining area. On the dining table are wrapped presents. "Ah, there she is!" my dad exclaims, getting up from his chair, coffee cup in hand. "The birthday girl!"

"Bald old man," my tics go.

Mai runs up to me and throws her arms around my waist, she just about reaches my stomach. "Imma sing for you!" she says excitedly, her ginger hair shining in the morning sun peeking through the window. She starts singing "Happy Birthday" to me. Jumping up and down, doing a dance she's making up at the spot. Once she's done, I sit down at the dining table. My mom puts my scrambled egg and toast in front of me on the disposable plate. My tics whistle and humph. I grab my plastic fork.

My dad shoves his birthday present in my face the second I've finished eating. It's flat and floppy. "I wanted to give you this to show you how much we support and love you, okay?" he goes dead serious, which makes me nervous. I let out a long "Okay." And give him a suspicious side-eye.

I rip the bright purple paper and can immediately tell what it is. Bright colors, oranges, pinks, and purples. I almost want to cry. It's a pride flag. I drop it into my lap, pouting my lips and sniffing. I smile at my parents. A little over a year ago I had come out to my parents. I cried and sobbed, scared of their reaction but they immediately embraced me and told me they'd love me no matter what. They also told me they had been suspecting it for a while. My dad makes his way over to me and hugs me tight. "Thank you so much."

Jana comes running over to me from one of the benches outside the school. I chuckle as I watch her get closer. Her brown hair flies in the wind, her heterochromia eyes lit up by the sun. She throws

herself around me, hugging me slightly too tight.
"Happy birthday!" she says and squeezes me again. Once she releases, she looks at me and goes: "We're currently the same age for the coming five months!" She places her hands on her hips, standing on her tippy toes to make herself tall. I chuckle again, smiling at the girl I love so dearly. "I got you a present!" she says as we walk over the schoolyard. The weather is starting to change, getting slightly warmer. I tilt my head at her. "You didn't have to do that."

"I know I didn't, but I did anyway!"

She grabbles into her bag and an oddly shaped present appears, wrapped in sage green. I carefully take it and rip the paper. I look at the plush, appreciating all of it. It's a turtle. I smile at Jana my heart does a little dance in my chest. "Thank you so much."

"You said you liked turtles," she goes, leaning forward, her hands intertwined behind her back.

"I sure do! Thank you so much, Jana." I give her a kiss on the cheek and squeeze her closer to me. Our cheeks press against each other.

Jana

"I heard you've been talking to Ellie quite a lot," the school counselor. Ms. Laurence goes as she smiles and leans forward. I nod and fidget with the sleeve of my beige crewneck. "Does it feel good?" she continues. I simply nod again. "I think that's wonderful Jana." I simply smile. "I think that's so good." Her eyes stare right into mine. “I-“ I manage to get out, she doesn’t budge or flinch. “I think I’ve been making progress,” I rattle out then inhale and hold my breath. “You definitely have been,” her voice sounds soft. I let out my breath and smile once again. “Yeah,” I mutter through my smile.

I sit at the trashcan table with Ellie, she’s eating her lunch as I just sit and watch, listening when she talks. The smell of a mixture of food infiltrates my nose, even just the scent of it makes me want to vomit, kinds of pasta and fatty fries. I look up only to see Liam walking over to us. I want to let out the biggest sigh ever but, instead, I look at Ellie, and I wish to hide away behind her. She looks at me, then at him, and sighs for the both of us. “Moo!” Liam bullies me. Leaning forward, smirking, and being trailed by a group of stupid teenage boys. “Fuck off Liam!” Ellie yells (not her tics.) My eyes widen and I force my smile down, trying not to laugh. “Shut up spaz!” He spits at Ellie. My eyebrows fury. Fuck this. “Oi, are you deaf? She said fuck off!” I yell, my heart sinks in my chest but Ellie laughing beside me makes my fear disappear. I look at her and laugh too before turning back to Liam. I can see Liam’s puzzled face. I bet he did not expect that.

I walk around the flower shop taking in the smell of wisteria, roses, and early tulips. I’ve always liked going to flower shops in winter. They give me such spring nostalgia. I try to find the perfect bouquet. The bouquet that says: "Dear Ellie, you've changed my life, thank you."

The door opens and Ellie's pretty face appears. She smiles at me first then her eyes go down to the bouquet of seven perfect red poppies. I decided that poppies would be best. Not roses, roses are simple. Ellie is anything but simple. She's different yet beautiful. She is my poppy in a world full of roses. She stands out, she's special. She smiles at me and tilts her head. "Jana!" she whines happily. I smile and hold the bouquet out to her. She grabs it and thanks me.

Ellie flops the poppies into a glass vase and nestles it on her windowsill. "I like your flag." I point at the sunset pride flag. Her tics whistle and she jerks her neck. She smiles at me and shrugs.

Her bed is slightly too small for two people, but we've managed to both get on there. She lays flat out. My left leg drapes over her right one. My head is supported by my hand, my hand is supported by my elbow, and my elbow is supported by the mattress below. We laugh and talk. We *talk*. About everything and nothing and I love every single conversation we have.

A comfortable silence falls, I take in her features, her ginger curls, and the million freckles on her cheeks. Her lips rose and oh so kissable. "Ellie?" I go softly. She looks over to me, staring straight into my eyes and I might just drown. I hesitate for a second. I readjust myself and lean into her, making my lips brush hers for a second. She blinks once at me. She pushes herself upright, her hand goes to my cheek, and she kisses me. The corner of my mouth perks up into a smile. Her lips really are kissable.

Ellie

Jana and I walk over the schoolyard, our hands intertwined. We laugh and joke and do all the things we're supposed to do. "Hey!" I hear an all too familiar voice. Jana and I both come to a stop and turn around to see Stephanie waving me over, her long black hair in a high sleek ponytail, it still reaches halfway her back. I scoff. "Let's go," Jana whispers to me, her breath soft on my neck, and squeezes my hand. "Yeah," I say shortly, and we continue on. "Oh! Yeah!" We can hear her yell. I tic and jerk. "Go follow cowgirl over here!" I can feel Jana's hand tense in mine. We both come to a stop and turn towards the girl I called my friend again, my head's blank, I want to punch Steph in the face but instead... "Fuck off Steph!" I yell out to her, loud and clear, my lungs filled with anger. She comes closer. "What?" she goes. "So, you two are friends now?" she pauses for a moment, her eyes darting to our intertwined hands. "Oh!" she goes, throwing her hands up and landing on her thighs as she leans forward. "They're girlfriends, huh?" She mocks us. I scoff.

Steph's gaze shifts from me to Jana. "What?" She takes a step closer to her. Jana's hands grow sweaty and tighter. "Stephanie, leave us alone." I nudge Jana and we walk on. Hoping Stephanie will leave us be. "Ellie!" Steph yells, making my twitch end humph. "She's just using you!" I try to shut her out, close my eyes and grind my teeth, but she just keeps going. "You really think she likes you!? You think she thinks you're just the most amazing girl she's ever met?"

I turn around, releasing Jana's hand. "Shut up!"

"Because when she sees you twitch and tic, she just can't help herself?"

"Shut up!" I scream.

"She just wants someone to hide behind, so she doesn't get bullied!"

"Shut up!" Jana's voice pierces through the air. Stephanie takes a step back in disbelief. "I like Ellie!" she yells out. "I like her because she's the kindest and bravest and most beautiful girl out there, inside, and out! So shut up!"

I take Jana's hand again. "Let's go, we don't need this shit." I drag Jana with me, taking one last glance at the girl I once trusted.

"Agreed," she simply says.

March

Ellie

It's late into the night. Jana and I giggle and laugh. The room is lit up by fairy lights, making the vines in her room look all the more magical. I roll onto my side, my right cheek squashed into the soft green fluffy blanket. I smile at her; I smile at the girl with the heterochromia eyes and birthmark. I look at her and see all the good in the world.

Jana rolls over and grabs a bright yellow polaroid camera from the nightstand. She seems to have painted daisies all over it. She rolls back over to me. Holding the camera high above us, I smile at the lens giving it a peace sign. The camera clicks and flashes so brightly that I might've just gone blind. I blink a few times, "Jesus!" I exclaim. "You just blinded me." Jana chuckles and takes the film off of the top, the picture is still nothing but whiteness. I lay my hand on her cheek and gently kiss those soft lips.

The sun shines through my eyelids, making everything look burnt orange. I yawn and stretch my body. My feet touch Jana's leg and I almost shiver. She's still sound asleep beside me. I sleepily sit up and scratch through my hair before getting up and walking over to the window. I open the blinds and take in the early spring day. Then turn around and make my way over to the other side of the bed, kneeling down beside the girl I like oh so much. I stare at her perfect imperfections and brush a strand of hair away from her face. I peck her cheek.

Above us, the sky is in its navy form, and the cars are dimly illuminated by the street lanterns, giving it that eerie end-of-the-world-apocalypse vibe. I listen to the sound of our footsteps, sounding scratchy on the brick pave walk beneath us. It's mostly quiet, though when passing bushes, there's the sound of crickets chirping. Even my tics stay silent. We round a corner; in the distance, I can hear the thumping of a bass. I come to a sharp stop, Jana trails a few steps further, stopping as she notices I'm no longer beside her. I relax my head and shoulders, giving her that "well that's not what I thought we'd be doing tonight" kind of look. A smile creeps up on her face. I sigh. "I'd rather have you lure me to my death than you lure me to a house party," I say softly. She sighs and locks her elbow into mine. "You're a freshman in high school," she goes. "You need to have gone to at least one house party when a freshman."

I tilt my head at her, throwing her an annoyed glare. She sighs loudly and groans. "See it as an initiation," she pauses. "A hazing!" I groan again and lazily continue walking following the music.

The sound of the bass thumps the loudest through the walls. In front of the house, there are a few teenagers in the front yard. There's a group of boys by the window, they're holding red plastic cups. At the edge, there's a girl throwing up while another girl holds her hair out of the way. There's whooping and shouting from inside. I jiggle my leg and chew on the sleeve of my sage green sweater. I look around the street, this does not seem like a good idea. I can see an old man standing on his front lawn a few houses down the road. He has that pissed off I'm-about-to-call-the-police look on his face. Jana nudges me with her elbow. "You'll be fine" she tries to comfort me. I smile a nervous smile. "Come on," she says softly, and we walk towards the entrance of the big suburban house.

It doesn't take long for me to lose Jana out of sight.

I find my way into the kitchen; the music is hurting my ears and the air reeks of alcohol and cigarette smoke. I should definitely not be here. I step onto my tippy toes, looking through the huge crowd of dancing, drunk teenagers. I can't seem to spot her anywhere. I bite my fingernails, eying the crowd continuously, hoping her face pops up. "Hey there," a teenage boy stumbles over to me, he seems to be at least a year older than me. I take a step back as my face freezes. My back softly thuds against the wall behind me. Grinding my teeth, my eyes dart from his to the floor. "You all alone here?"

He yells over the music. He's drunk and his eyes are narrowed, half-open at best. He's high *and* drunk and I'm uncomfortable. I shift but my feet are rooted in the ground and scan the crowd again but there's still no sign of Jana. "Here," the boy goes. "Have a beer," he goes and shoves a dark-tinted beer bottle into my hands. It looks like one of those cheap ones that are a dollar less expensive than the good ones. Not that I know what the good ones are, I don't drink. "So, what you up to?" He continues to bother me. I'm sure he means no harm but I'm still uncomfortable. I scan the crowd once again and notice her instantly, her birthmark. My heart calms down again. "Let me get your number," the drunk boy says. I take a final look at him. "Sorry, I'm a lesbian," I shrug and make my way over to Jana. I grab her hand. "I lost you!" she yells as I guide her up the stairs.

We make our way into the bathroom. The door closes and the music gets muffled, I can still feel the bass thumping through the floor. I turn the lock, sigh deeply and take a seat on the cold tile floor of the small bathroom and Jana does the same. The room feels almost clinical. White all over. It smells fresh though, like citrus. I look at the beer bottle in my hand and chuckle. "A dude offered me a beer."

"It's still closed right?" she goes.

I feel the tab. "Yep."

"Well then we'll share!" she grabs the bottle from my hand, takes off the tab with her bare teeth, and takes a sip before handing it back to me. I also give it a sip and cringe at the taste in my mouth. "No thank you," I mumble trying to get the taste of my mouth. Jana laughs. "So how are you liking your first house party?"

I shrug. "It's loud, scary and it quite literally stinks." Jana chuckles again. I tilt my head at her, taking in all of her beauty once again. I shrug. "I'd much rather just be with you."

She smiles shyly, getting from her butt onto her knees and slides over the sit next to me. Her soft hand touches my cheek, making me almost shiver. She leans in and I close my eyes, letting those kissable lips touch mine. "You taste like beer," I say and chuckle. "Bleh," I go. We both laugh. The doorknob shudders, making us both jump up. There's loud knocking and then a voice sounds. "Get out! I need to fucking pee!" We both laugh before getting up, Jana takes my hand as we walk out the door, letting the hurried girl go inside. "Let's go home," Jana says.

April

Ellie

The warmth of the sun embraces my skin. I stretch out my body, the sheets make a scratchy sound. The thin blanket only covers my right leg and a bit of my back. The weather has become nicer. Everything is waking up, the trees and flowers, the birds, and butterflies. The bees have begun their annual pollination. I groan softly, open my eyes, and yawn. There are rows of light illuminating my wall from where they creep through the cracks in my blinds. I manage to get myself upright. The floor of my room is covered in clothes and on my desk, there's a pile of homework. Dust dances in the sun's rays. Slowly floating around the air. I put one foot out of bed, then the other. The sun has warmed up my wooden floor. I readjust my tank top and pull up my shorts just over my belly button. I look at the little frog statue on my bedside table. Its arms reach out above its head. Little slits in its hands, holding a polaroid of Jana and me that we made not too long ago. I smile stupidly, thinking about her. There's a soft "ting" from my phone, I stretch myself out once again before grabbing my phone. I smile at her name. We exchange good morning texts every morning. I tap with my thumbs and send her a good morning back. Today we're going on a date.

The bookstore smells sort of stuffy. That's to be expected. The enormous number of books have that kind of smell. Maybe it's also because dust has slowly settled on them. Jana's hand is kind of sweaty in mine, but I don't mind. She smells extra good today, like lavender and wisteria, I guess she put on perfume today. We just kind of shuffle around, strolling slowly. This Barnes and Noble is quite big, the books are neatly placed on the shelves. Some lean against each other only showing their spine. A few of the same, then that one but the cover in view. I look at all the Colleen Hoover books, TikTok's been raging about those. Jana squeezes my hand and I come to a stop. "Hmm?" I go, looking into her beautiful heterochromia eyes. "Let's pick out books for each other," she smiles. I smile back and nod.

Jana

There's a mix match of tables. All different sizes and all made of different woods. Some are even black. Some look old and vintage. I continue strolling down the shop, trying to find the perfect book to give Ellie. I had asked her before what she likes in a book. She said she loves fantasy books and said: "I'm a sucker for the "enemies to lovers" trope." I agreed with her. I scan the shop, seeing if I can spot her. She's in the corner, scrolling through a book. Her red hair seems to be even fierier in the lighting of the shop. I smile stupidly.

There are three small squared black tables, forming a kind of crisscross pattern with each other. All of them have a sign that reads “BookTok’s Favorites.” I make that my spot and look at all the books they have to offer. There are many of Colleen Hoover’s books. *It Ends with Us, Ugly Love, All Your Perfects*, and a few others.
I decide to leave the TikTok section.

I decide on the first book in *Julie Kagawa’s “Talon”* series.

We sit down at the coffee shop; the sky outside is slowly darkening. I place the paper bag with our books down beside the table. Ellie hides her face behind her hands. She looks cute when she’s shy. I smile at her. “You’re so pretty,” I mutter. There’s a soft muffled chuckle before she removes her hands. “You’re the prettiest,” she simply goes. A young woman, dressed in a green apron strolls over to us. She has sharp cheekbones, and her hair is tied up in a high ponytail. “What will it be for the ladies?” she goes and holds her tiny notepad ready. My heart rate increases. I can do this. I tell myself. Nope, I can’t. I give Ellie a quick look and she knows exactly what it means. “I’ll have a caramel macchiato,” she looks from the young woman back to me. She smiles at me before shifting her gaze back to the waiter. “And my girlfriend will have an iced matcha latte.”
The waiter smiles at both of us and simply goes: “Okeydokey.”

Ellie

My feet move fast below me as they shuffle on the concrete below. I make my way over to the two girls I used to call my friends. I can't take it any longer, I just need some kind of closure. They both sit on one of the concrete tables in the schoolyard. My feet bring me closer to the two girls until they come to a stop in front of them. They look up at me from their conversation. Miriam smiles quickly. I take a deep breath and turn my gaze to Stephanie. "Steph, what you did was a shitty thing, and afterward you only made it worse," I rattle out, kind of like word vomit. She rolls her eyes at me, and I almost want to turn around again and leave. "I know you meant no harm when posting that video." Her sheepish eyes look up at me. "But it still hurt my feelings." She slowly shakes her head. "I told you that I'm sorry and you just ignore it."

I take another deep breath and dust off my hands on my black shorts. "Steph," I go. "I forgive you."

Miriam's eyebrows perk up. "But damn, you've been a mean girl!" I say loudly. Steph laughs. "Why are you so *obsessed* with me?!" she roars with dramatic gestures. I laugh at her reference. Steph straightens herself again. "I really meant no harm," she bows down her head as if too scared to face me. "And I'm sorry I was nasty about Jana," she takes a deep shaky breath. "I just didn't want her to steal you away from me." I look into Steph's icy blue eyes and then shift my gaze to Miriam. She smiles a crooked smile before getting onto her feet and embracing me. I hold her back. “I missed you,” her muffled voice sounds. “I missed you too.”

“Should I be jealous?” an all too familiar voice sounds behind me. I loosen my grip on Miriam and turn to look at Jana. “Not at all,” I say rather seductively. I hop over to her and kiss her pretty lips. I look back at the two girls. “There is a catch though,” I go. “Jana joins the friend group.”

“Welcome, Jana!” Steph exclaims loudly.

May

Jana

One step forward, two steps back.

Thursday

My mom had been rushing, grabbing anything we might need. Feeds, extra clothing, and my medication. She rushed me to the car; I wasn't all there. I knew my mom was panicking, and part of me was too but, my mind was in a purgatory state. I know I was fearful, but my hazy mind didn't care all that much. My mom got in on the other side, only to realize she forgot her keys. She sighed deeply and placed her hands on her temples before rushing back into the house to go grab them. I don't remember much of the trip to the hospital. My temperature was 101.3 that early morning. My sweating was terrible, my hair sticking to my forehead, and my skin was almost transparent. Yet I was shivering and freezing.

In the hospital, they figured out my GJ-tube had an infection.

I sob again. Pleading with my eyes to my mother. I just want it to stop. My mom is shushing me, stroking my cheek, petting it while squeezing my hand tightly. "I'm in so much pain, my tube is hurting."

"I know hun," my mom says as she wipes the sticky hairs from my sweaty face. "The pain meds aren't helping!" I continue sobbing and getting out of breath. But with every sob a pain radiates through my stomach, making me want to crawl up into a ball and just not exist. "I want Ellie!" I yell out, continuing sobbing as I turn my head away from my mom.

Friday

I shed the slumber from my brain quicker than usual. It doesn't take long for me to awaken. Anyone would with all the beeping around them and wires and tubes attached at every point on their body. I lift my hands to my forehead, the wires pulling and tugging from all over. The pain is a lot better than the day before. My mom is sleeping on the chair in the corner, it's a light medic blue, making the room look all that much more clinical. They could've gone for a happier color. Maybe a bright yellow or a nice purple. Her fluffy jacket is pulled over her body like a blanket, she is completely still, nothing moving apart of her stomach going up and down at every breath. The sky is starting to brighten up, but the sun has not yet reached the horizon. I look at the clock above the door of the cold pale hospital room. It's five in the morning.

I watch the drip on the IV bag, I watch it drip single drops of antibiotics into my system. The pain is getting better. I don't know if it's because they've been pumping pain medication into me or if the antibiotics are working. I've been boredly watching movies on the small hospital tv that rests on the wall opposite my bed. It's hard to focus on what the people on the screen are saying. The hospital is loud and busy. Apart from the beeping of all the machines and the automatic blood pressure machine around my arm that puffs up every ten or so minutes, clasping tight around my biceps before releasing with a big sigh, there's the commotion in the hallways. A collection of beeping noises, the elevator that dings every once in a while, and busy nurses over speakers calling for doctors with all kinds of names. The shuffling of hygienic white sneakers bothers me the most, squeaking over the tile floors as the nurses make their rounds around the rooms.

Night falls again, the twilight lingers on the horizon behind the city buildings, and the field with trees has already darkened into a night setting, making it look eerie. The sky is lighter up above than it is on the horizon and the long clouds are a dark blueish-grey color. The moon is slightly visible in its waxing state. The days are boring. I'm smelly from not having showered the last few days. At least tomorrow Ellie is visiting. And that's always a good thing.

Saturday

I wince in pain as the doctor loosens my tube, moving slightly upwards but quickly letting my body relax back down. I grind my teeth for a second and narrow my eyes. My tube had to be loosened because it was becoming too tight around my skin with all the swelling from the infection. "It's done," he goes and stands up from the little round stool. Taking off his latex white gloves and throwing them in the yellow medical waste bin. He disinfects his hands with the suspender that's mounted on the wall beside my bed. I breathe heavily as tears sting the corners of my eyes. "We're going to come back to rotate and advance your tube maybe today or tomorrow, just to make sure it won't cause any further complications because we did see on the scan that it is backing up a bit."

"Will that hurt like a son of a bitch too?"

"We'll give you a sedation," the doctor simply nods and walks out.

I look at my mom and sigh deeply before dropping my head on the pillow. "I think it's best if Ellie comes by a different time, or when you're out of the hospital."

"What?" I exclaim, sitting up fast. "Honey, you're really sick, I don't think it's a good idea."

I take a deep breath and slowly blow it out. "I absolutely hate this mom." My body fills with sadness and tightness. I suppress my tears. "I know honey."

Midday has passed and the pain has only increased. I'm sobbing and crying and wincing in pain. My mom tries to comfort me, but nothing is helping. I breathe slowly, hoping the pain will pass.

Sunday

It's so early in the morning that the sky is still in a nighttime setting. Navy blue, illuminated with a countless number of stars, the moon is no longer in view, the earth has turned away from her. My mom is once again sleeping on the clinical blue couch in the corner with her makeshift coat blanket. The first thing I notice is that the pain is significantly better than the days before. There's a slight bit of aching and I no longer feel like I'm going to shiver so hard I might break my teeth over it. Tomorrow finals start. I won't be there for it. I've always been able to manage it somehow, my illness, and my school. But the last school year has been my toughest yet. But it has somehow also been my best yet. Maybe I'll double my year. I might be in some of Ellie's classes if I did. I blink tiredly, I might as well sleep a bit longer.

I watch the nurse put the glass tube on the syringe, the blood seeps into it quickly. Her pale blue latex gloves make an icky noise as they rub against each other. She takes it off and flips it upside down back upright. Then takes another one. If the inflammation levels in my blood have gone down and stabilized, I might be allowed to go home today.

Another nurse comes in for the third time today to clean the drainage around my GJ-tube.

Bad news. Again. My lab results showed that my infection levels have gone up again.

There's a knock on my hospital door. I groan. "Again, with the nurses!" I say annoyed and shift to my side, fiddling into a comfortable position which is near impossible with all these wires. I can hear the door open. "Someone ordered a taxi?" an all too familiar voice sounds. I jump up and look at the ginger-haired girl. "Ellie!" I say excitedly. She rolls a wheelchair into the room. But leaves it behind halfway, pushing it to the side. She throws her arms around me, and I hold her so tightly, tight enough that she'll never be able to leave. "The doctor said I can take you on a walk with a wheelchair." Her muffled voice sounds. I let her go, smiling at the girl I like oh so much. "Well let's go! I'm getting tired from laying here all day!"

Ellie wheels me around the garden behind the hospital, in front of the too-perfect trees. I haven't laughed since I came in last Thursday. "You're a safety hazard!" I yell at her as she zooms me around.

Monday

It's almost midday again. My pain has eased a lot and I think part of it is because of Ellie. She is honestly my light upon the hill. The doctor walks in. "Good news, your inflammation levels have gone down, and you'll be discharged later today." He smiles at me, but it's one of those forced once, one of these I-either-have-to-look-pitiful-or-pretend-to-be-happy smiles. But I'll take it.

The nurse walks in for the last time. It's a young lady with long brownish-blond hair tied in a high ponytail. She unhooks me from all the machines going around me. I count at first but after wire six I decide I don't even want to know. Lastly, she carefully takes out my IV. I watch her pull it straight out, quickly covering the puncture hole with a cotton ball. "Hold it please," her polite voice sounds, and I press down on the cotton ball with my index and middle finger. I wait for a few seconds as she cleans up before she removes my hand and band-aids the puncture hole. My mom grabs a pile of fresh clothes for me to get into instead of this annoying stinky hospital gown. "What's the first thing you'll do when you get home?"

"Take a fucking shower," I breathe out.

"Understandable," my mom chuckles.

"Freedom!" I yell out as my mom wheels me through those big doors. I'm finally going home.

I walk through the school hallway, passing by students, all of them different, all of them with different fears, wishes, and things they love. Each of them is unique. I make my way to the school cafeteria. I keep my head up high. My GJ-tube peeks out from below my shirt, rubbing against the skin of my stomach, the tube going into my backpack where my feed is kept. I'm tired of hiding. No one should ever hide.

Ellie is waiting for me at the entrance. I grab her hand, not saying a single word, and drag her to the middle of the cafeteria. Stephanie gives us a confused look as we pass by her and Miriam. I let Ellie's hand slip out of mine, set one foot on the bench, then the other, standing tall on the table. It feels unsteady below me, quivering with every slight move I make. My heart is pounding, but I have to do this. I already caught the attention of a few people. They're all murmuring to each other, pointing. I take a deep breath and look at Ellie for a split second, she looks confused, yet intrigued, turning her head in a slight pitch. I smile widely. "Here's the tea!" I yell out, and the chattering of people quiets down. Confused faces turn my way. "There's only one thing we all want," I start. "It is to be accepted for who we are." I scan the cafeteria, looking a few people in the eyes. "We need to celebrate our differences instead of bullying those who aren't like us." My eyes meet Ellie's for a second. I scan the room again and catch the eyes of Miss Laurence. She smiles, winks, and nods. "I am human, like all of you. Yes, I have gastroparesis, and I happen to have a feeding tube. I have a birthmark that covers almost half of my face." I take another breath. "But I am human. Disability isn't a choice, but acceptance is. Be who you are and be fucking proud of it."

Ellie takes a leap, coming to a stand beside me. I look into her eyes as she looks into mine. "You are badass," she says, lays her hands on my cheeks, and kisses me. Once we part, she chuckles. She takes a few steps back and raises her hands above her head before yelling out: "I am disabled and proud!" she shouts at the top of her lungs. "I am bisexual and proud!" A voice sounds from the crowd. "I am autistic and proud!" another one goes. "I am black and proud!"

We should all be proud. Cause at the end of the day, we are who we are. We all grow at different paces. And maybe you aren't a rose about to bloom, maybe you're a poppy. Different but still beautiful, beautiful, but different. Be proud. Accept each other.
We should all learn:

Disability isn't a choice, acceptance is.

What a journey!

Words from the author:

Hi there! I'm Phoebe Jacobs, the author behind this novella. I started writing this during a period in my life when my chronic illnesses were posing a significant impact on my life. Writing this novella became an outlet for me to navigate the overwhelming challenges I faced. I truly enjoyed writing Jana's and Ellie's story. I myself struggle with Tourette Syndrome and wanted to show some insight into how Tourette's can impact someone's life. I want to show that disability isn't a choice, but that acceptance is.

I would like to let you know that Ellie's case of Tourette's is pictured quite severe. Most people's Tourette Syndrome isn't this severe and all cases present different. Tourette's is a spectrum, with each case being unique in its expression and impact on individuals.

In exploring Jana's struggles with Gastroparesis, I did my best to educate myself through research and conversations with individuals living with Gastroparesis. Please keep in mind that perhaps not everything is medically accurate.

Want to learn more about Jana's and Ellie's conditions? I summarized some information for you on the following pages!

However, it is imperative to clarify that this content is offered for informational purposes and is not intended to serve as a diagnostic guide. If you suspect that you may be experiencing symptoms related to these conditions, I strongly advise seeking guidance from a qualified medical professional for a proper evaluation and guidance.

Sincerely,
Phoebe Jacobs

Selective Mutism:

Selective mutism is an anxiety disorder where a person is unable to speak in certain social situations, such as with classmates at school or to relatives they do not see very often. It usually starts during childhood and, if left untreated, can persist into adulthood.

A child or adult with selective mutism does not refuse or choose not to speak at certain times, they're literally unable to speak.

The expectation to talk to certain people triggers a freeze response with feelings of anxiety and panic, and talking is impossible.

In time, the person may learn to anticipate the situations that provoke this distressing reaction and do all they can to avoid them.

However, people with selective mutism are able to speak freely to certain people, such as close family and friends, when nobody else is around to trigger the freeze response.

Selective mutism affects about 1 in 140 young children. It's more common in girls and children who have recently migrated from their country of birth.

Gastroparesis:

Gastroparesis, also called delayed gastric emptying or stomach paralysis, is a disorder that slows or stops the movement of food from your stomach to your small intestine, even though there is no blockage in the stomach or intestines.

Gastroparesis is thought to be a problem with the nerves and muscles in the stomach. It's not always known what causes it.

It can be a complication of long-term conditions such as diabetes, EDS, etc...

Gastroparesis can also be a complication after some types of surgery.

Symptoms of gastroparesis start after eating and may include:

- feeling full sooner than usual – you may be unable to finish meals.
- feeling sick and being sick
- tummy pain
- heartburn
- bloating

Tourette Syndrome:

Tourette Syndrome (TS) is a condition of the nervous system. TS causes people to have "tics". Tics are sudden twitches, movements, or sounds that people make repeatedly. People who have tics cannot stop their bodies from doing these things. For example, a person might keep blinking over and over.

It usually starts during childhood, but the tics and other symptoms usually improve after several years and sometimes go away completely.

There's no cure for Tourette's syndrome, but treatment can help manage symptoms.

People with Tourette's syndrome may also have obsessive-compulsive disorder (OCD), attention deficit hyperactivity disorder (ADHD), or learning difficulties.

Obsessive-compulsive disorder

Obsessive-compulsive disorder (OCD) is a common mental health condition where a person has obsessive thoughts and compulsive behaviors. OCD can affect men, women, and children. Some people start having symptoms early, often around puberty, but it usually starts during early adulthood.

Check out Phoebe Jacobs' earlier work!

Published by BoekScout
ISBN: 978-94-643-1419-9

About the author.

Phoebe Jacobs is a writer from a small town in Belgium.

Her passion for storytelling dates back to her childhood years.

Commencing her literary journey at the age of thirteen, Phoebe achieved a significant milestone with the publication of her debut novel, "Kissing in Swimming Pools," in 2021 at the age of nineteen.

Her writing focuses on exploring significant life themes such as mental health, bullying, sexuality, gender identity, and disability—themes inspired by her personal experiences. Through her work, Phoebe aims to shed light on these crucial topics, raise awareness, and support those who go through similar experiences.

Printed in Great Britain
by Amazon

48569980R00067